The Millionaire's Seductive Revenge

MAXINE SULLIVAN

™ MILLS & BOON®

Pure reading pleasure

First published in Great Britain 2008
Large Print edition 2008
Silhouette Books Limited, Eton House,
18-24 Paradise Road, Richmond, Surrey, TW9 1SR

© Maxine Sullivan 2007

ISBN: 978 0 263 20114 7

Set in Times Roman 17¼ on 21 pt.
36-0308-42877

Printed and bound in Great Britain
by Antony Rowe Ltd, Chippenham, Wiltshire

MAXINE SULLIVAN

credits her mother for her lifelong love of romance novels, so it was a natural extension to want to write her own romances that she and others could enjoy. She's very excited about seeing her work in print, and she's thrilled to be the second Australian to write for the Desire line.

Maxine lives in Melbourne, Australia, but over the years has travelled to New Zealand, the U.K. and the U.S. In her own backyard, her husband's job ensured they saw the diversity of the countryside including spending many years in Darwin in the tropical north where some of her books are set. She is married to Geoff, who has proven his hero status many times over the years. They have two handsome sons and an assortment of much-loved previously abandoned animals.

Maxine would love to hear from you, and she can be contacted through her website at www.maxinesullivan.com

For Andrea Johnston,
Suzanne Barrett and
Nolene Jenkinson,
Critique Partners, Mentors
and Friends

One

Every man in the room was staring at Kia Benton. And Brant Matthews was one of them. He'd seen many beautiful women in his life but none who affected him like the woman who'd entered the ballroom of Darwin's Shangri-La Hotel. Australia's most northerly city may possess a tropical lifestyle that was the envy of the rest of the country, but it still didn't hold a candle to this woman's beauty.

Dressed for an evening that promised glitz

and glamour, Kia looked stunning tonight, with her ash-blond hair pulled back in a stylish chignon, her perfectly made-up features accentuated by the black liner circling her eyes.

The eyes of a seductress, Brant mused, his gaze sliding down over bare shoulders to the shimmery silver dress that hugged her breasts, then slid over slim hips and long legs.

But it wasn't just her looks that coiled sexual hunger in the pit of his stomach. She had something that called to him on another level. A quality he'd never found in another woman, not even in his ex-fiancée, Julia. Hell, definitely not Julia. Julia had only been about one thing.

His mouth tightened. He had to remember that Kia was no different. Both women wanted the same thing.

Money.

He'd been suspicious of Kia from the moment he'd stepped onto the plane on his way back from Europe and caught sight of a photograph of her and his partner Phillip in the society section of a Darwin magazine. It was being read by the man next to him, and the picture had shown her arm in arm with Phillip at a cocktail party, looking very pleased with herself. The last he heard, Phillip still had his secretary from years back. This Kia was a total shock.

The caption had read, "Has one of Australia's richest bachelors finally been hooked by his new personal assistant? Miss Kia Benton obviously knows a thing or two about getting 'personal.'"

Yes, this woman knew how to get her hooks into someone all right. But what she didn't know was that he'd heard her on the telephone when he'd gone into the office the next day.

Of course I'm working on getting myself a rich man, she'd been saying when he'd passed by Phillip's office and seen her leaning against the desk, looking for all the world as if she owned the place. Then she'd laughed and said, *It's as easy to love a rich man as a poor one, right?*

This was the reason she'd made herself indispensable to his business partner so quickly. Within two months she'd had Phillip eating out of her hand. Oh, yes, she was a gold digger, this one. A beautiful, deceitful gold digger.

"Oh, don't they make a lovely couple?" one of the executive wives tossed into the conversation going on around him, pulling Brant from his thoughts and dropping him back into the Christmas festivities that were a necessary evil at this time of year.

"Yes, they're perfect together," one of the others agreed after all heads turned toward Kia and Phillip standing beneath the Merry Christmas sign in the doorway.

Then the head of the Legal Department's wife put her hand on her husband's arm. "Hon, I don't know what they're putting in the water at your office, but she's beautiful."

Simon puffed up with an odd sort of

fatherly pride. "That's Kia. She's got brains as well as beauty."

Brains as well as beauty.

And she had no qualms about using those assets, Brant thought, hating the pull of her attraction but unable to do anything about it.

Dammit. If only he'd met her first. But two months ago, as senior partner, he'd gone to Paris to establish their new office and get everything up and running. Phillip hadn't wanted to go because he'd been heavily involved with his then girlfriend, Lynette. Yet when he'd returned a month later, Phillip's secretary had resigned due to ill health and Kia had been firmly ensconced as Phillip's personal assistant during work hours.

And his constant companion out of hours.

Like now.

Of course, if he'd seen her first, they would have been lovers straight away. No doubt about it. He'd known it from the moment he'd gazed into her sparkling aquamarine eyes.

Why?

Because she knew what she did to him, that's why. She knew the attraction he felt for her. This deep, pulsing need to make her his own. She merely had to glance his way and sizzling heat coursed through his veins. Even now he could feel himself burning to be inside her, feeling her close around him as he moved ever so slowly in and out, watching her eyelids flutter against her cheeks, hearing his name a murmur on the parted bow of her lips.

"She's got a brand new car, too," someone interrupted his thoughts, making him stiffen in disbelief. "A Porsche. It's fantastic."

"Lucky girl," one of the guys said. "Did Phil buy it for her?"

Simon darted a look at Brant, as if he knew this wasn't a subject they should be discussing in front of the boss. "Er…I'm not sure," the other man said awkwardly.

"It's understandable," Simon's wife added in

a sympathetic tone. "He probably doesn't want her to have a similar accident to the one he had."

Pretending to ignore the conversation, Brant leaned back in his chair and took a sip of his whiskey. Late one night, Phil's car had broken down after he'd gone out on a date with Kia. When he'd stepped out to check the problem, a passing vehicle had clipped his leg, busting up his knee and breaking his ankle, leaving him with what would eventually be a permanent limp.

And Kia…God bless her, Brant mused cynically…had been quite happy ever since, going back and forth between the hospital and the office, assisting Phil with his workload. Through it all she must have been manipulating him to get the car. And a Porsche, to boot. Bloody hell. His friend and business partner deserved better than someone who was only using him for his bank account.

He was tempted to show Phil what sort of

woman he was involved with. Kia would be easy enough to get into bed if he really put his mind to it. Only he couldn't. Not for *her* sake but for Phillip's. He knew how it felt for someone close to steal your woman.

And he'd be damned if he'd put the business at risk. He may've had to correct some of Phillip's poor decisions since they'd started buying up other businesses three years ago, but the last thing Brant wanted was instability within the company that was now riding the wave of phenomenal success.

Yet all of it could be jeopardized because of a woman who was out to get everything she could, he reminded himself as he watched the pair moving through the tables toward him, Kia pushing Phil's wheelchair but stopping to talk to people on the way. Oh, she was good at what she did. She knew how to work her audience.

Sickened that such beauty hid a heart of

stone, Brant stood up. "Back in a minute," he muttered to no one in particular and headed for the exit behind him. His date had vanished into the nether regions of the ladies' room a while back, so he was unconcerned she would miss him until his return.

He needed to get outside and let the ocean air fill his lungs and clear away the smell of deception. Then maybe his body wouldn't ache so much for a woman who deserved nothing more than his contempt.

After finally reaching their table, Kia sat back with a glass of champagne and tried to relax. Brant seemed to have disappeared for a while, though she knew he'd be back. And he always affected her in some crazy way, no matter how hard she tried not to let him.

Tonight, for instance, it had started as soon as she entered the ballroom. She'd felt his eyes upon her, scrutinizing her, undressing her. This wasn't the only time she'd sensed his desire. Far from it. From the moment she'd met him she'd known he'd wanted her, despite himself. In his bed and out of it. Anywhere and anytime.

And as much as she had fought it, his want always bonded with a need deep inside her. That knowledge had pulsed through her veins tonight, making her breathless, wanting more, wanting him.

"Everything all right, Kia?"

She took a breath and fixed a smile on her lips for Phillip, fully aware of the attention from the other tables guests. "Everything's fine."

His gaze slid to her throat and a glint of humor appeared in his eyes. "I'm glad you like your present."

Her hand went to the sparkling diamond necklace he'd asked her to wear. He'd wanted her to keep it, but she'd refused, so they'd compromised and she'd said she'd wear it only for the night. "It's fabulous."

"A fabulous gift for a fabulous lady."

She shifted in her seat. Did he have to lay it on quite so thick? Just because he wanted to give the impression they were a couple didn't mean they should act like characters in a thirties melodrama. It made her uncomfortable.

Suddenly the hairs on the back of her neck began to rise. There Brant was, dancing with a woman at the far end of the dance floor. Her breath caught at the sight of him, desire shooting to every region in her body.

He was certainly something to look at. Handsome, wealthy, extremely sexy in a black suit that matched the color of his gleaming dark hair and fitted his lean body to perfection. He exuded an attraction she found difficult to deny.

"Who's that dancing with Brant?" a visitor to the table asked the question on Kia's mind.

"That's his date," someone replied.

Kia hid her surprise. Brant usually only

dated blondes. Beautiful blondes with gorgeous figures and impeccable style, if the photographs in the newspaper were anything to go by. Certainly the women who frequented his office were blond and beautiful. And according to Evelyn, his personal assistant, so were the women who called him constantly on the phone.

This brunette was definitely not in his league. The woman wasn't beautiful, though she wasn't unattractive either. She just lacked the confidence of those other women, and that red-and-white floral dress looked totally wrong on her. It seemed to swallow her up. Just as Brant's presence seemed to be doing.

And didn't she know how *that* felt, she scoffed to herself as the other woman smiled shyly up at him and Brant returned the smile with a devastating one of his own. The woman stumbled, and who could blame her? Brant Matthews, Womanizer Extraordinaire, had struck again. Maybe she could suggest he have that printed on his business cards.

All at once she realized Phillip had spoken. "Sorry, Phillip. What did you say?"

"I said she's my new physiotherapist."

Ah, so this was Serena. They'd spoken on the telephone. But why had *Brant* chosen her as his date? It didn't make sense.

Then it hit her.

"Phillip, you didn't," she said for his ears only.

"Didn't what?"

"Fix them up together."

He frowned. "Why not? I thought it would do Serena good to be asked out by someone like Brant. He didn't mind."

Oh, that poor girl. Why were men so insensitive at times?

"That's exactly why he's wrong for her."

His brows drew closer together. "What do you mean?"

"She'll know people will be wondering

what Brant sees in her and that'll make her feel even worse."

"I was only trying to help," he said a touch defensively.

Kia's heart softened. "I know you were. It's just that…" How to explain the mind of a shy, insecure woman? It wasn't easy delving into her own past and reliving her inadequacies.

"Merry Christmas, Kia."

Without warning, Brant was beside her, his lips brushing against her cheek in a gesture that meant nothing yet everything. Kia's pulse almost fell over itself as his warm hand touched her bare shoulder and she caught a whiff of his masculine scent. Her throat went dry.

Then he moved away and held the chair out for his date. "Serena, this is Kia, Phillip's personal assistant."

"We've spoken on the telephone," Kia said with a smile as the woman sat down opposite her.

"Oh, yes." The other woman gave a wavering

smile in return, and empathy stirred within Kia, helping her recover from the shock of Brant's greeting.

"Serena's a lovely name," Kia said, wanting to put her at ease.

Serena smiled tentatively. "You think so?"

"It suits you," Brant said before Kia could respond.

Serena blushed, looking quite pretty. "Thank you."

He sat down and handed her a glass of champagne. "Not too many women are as restful as you to be around, Serena."

Kia saw his eyes flick toward her. Was he saying *she* wasn't restful to be around? What a cheek. It wasn't her fault he wanted her but couldn't.

"Some men aren't restful to be around either," Kia pointed out, not willing to let him get the upper hand.

He eased back in his chair, confident but with

a dark look in his deep blue eyes that sent shivers down her spine. "Are you saying that some men disturb you, Kia?"

Was he asking if *he* disturbed her?

"People only disturb you if you let them. I don't ever intend to let any man disturb me."

"Really?" His eyes slid across to Phillip at her side, then back to her again. They hardened, reminding her that from the day he'd met up with her outside the hospital room after he'd returned from his trip, this man had grown more and more hostile toward her. He hid it well, but she knew it was there. She could only assume that because Phillip had been going home after a date with her, Brant blamed her for the accident.

And that was totally unfair, but she wasn't about to challenge him over it or he might start delving into her and Phillip's relationship and discover the truth. How it had all started when Phillip had begged her to be his partner at a business dinner with people who knew his ex, Lynette. Things had snowballed after that and now they were out of control. Totally out of control.

Glancing at Brant, she saw a muscle pulsating in his lean cheek. Then, as if he'd had enough of her, he turned away to talk to one of the others.

She felt a spurt of anger at his dismissal. Was this the way he treated women when he had enough of them? Did he use them to amuse himself, then get rid of them once they'd passed their use-by dates? Of course he did. So why did she feel surprised? Did she think she was any different just because she shared in this intense physical attraction?

Schooling her features, Kia sipped at her champagne and watched the couples dancing out on the floor. She could hear Phillip talking about going home to Queensland to be with his family for Christmas. It reminded her of her own plans to fly south to Adelaide to spend Christmas with her mother and stepfather. She was looking forward to having some downtime with her family. She badly needed time away from the office—and the men who ran it.

All at once, Phillip leaned forward and said loudly across the table, "Hey, Brant. How would you like to dance with Kia for me?"

"Wh-what?" Kia said before she could stop herself. She didn't want to be in Brant's arms. Close to him. Touching him.

Brant's eyes narrowed slightly, but was she the only one to see the flash of hunger in them? "Maybe Kia doesn't want to dance," he said, giving her an out, telling her that as much as he wanted her in his arms, another part of him didn't.

She managed a short laugh. "Phillip, don't be silly. I don't need to dance."

"I saw your foot tapping to the music," he said, surprising her because she hadn't been aware she'd been doing that.

She opened her mouth to say she really

didn't feel like dancing but then noticed all eyes upon her. Making a fuss would only make them wonder why she objected to dancing with Brant. And if that happened…

"Okay, Phillip. Anything for *you*," she emphasized, making sure Brant knew it wasn't for *him*.

And then, like a gentleman, Brant stood beside her, helping her out of her chair. She tried to smile, but already his closeness affected her. Every nerve in her body suddenly started to tingle as he led her out onto the dance floor and straight into his arms. Knowing she was in danger of melting against him, she stiffened and pulled back.

"We're only dancing," he mocked, knowing full well the effect he had on her.

On any woman.

On women in general.

"Mr. Matthews—"

His mouth thinned. "I've told you before. Call me Brant."

"You're my employer. I prefer to keep it formal."

"Why?"

"I was brought up to respect my elders."

His laughter was low and throaty, his lips showing the tip of perfect white teeth. *All the better to eat you with, my dear,* she thought.

He moved his hand more comfortably against the small of her back. "Thanks for putting me in my place."

"I try." She moved to dislodge his fingers. They were an inch too low for her liking.

"I know you do." He tilted his head. "It makes me wonder why."

She looked somewhere past his shoulder. "Because you're the boss."

His hand moved imperceptibly lower, snatching her breath away, drawing her eyes back to him. "If I'm the boss, then you should do what I say," he murmured, making the simple statement sound very, very personal.

Recovering, she squared her shoulders and lifted her chin. She was beginning to feel as if she were some sort of puppet to be manipulated. "I never *was* good at doing what I was told."

"Shame." His eyes hardened. "But I bet you know how to get your own way now."

"Doesn't everyone?" she quipped, not sure where this was heading.

"Every *woman,* you mean."

Ah, so the womanizer had a low opinion of women. Color her surprised.

"Actually, I meant every *person.* Man. Woman. Child. Even animals—"

"I hear you've got a new car," he cut across her. "A Porsche."

Her mind reeled in confusion, not only at what he'd said but at the hint of accusation in his tone, though what she was being accused of she had no idea.

"Yes, I do have a new car."

His lips twisted with a touch of cynicism. "We must be paying you well."

His animosity was growing in leaps and bounds. "You get what you pay for," she pointed out coolly.

"I'm sure we do." He leaned closer so that his lips were practically pressed to her ear. "Or should I say *Phil* gets what he paid for."

She stiffly drew back. "What do you mean by that?"

The corners of his mouth curved in a smooth smile that didn't match the piercing glint in his eyes. "Merely that you're a top-notch PA. I'm sure Phil believes he's lucky to have you."

"That sounds like a backhanded compliment."

"Does it?" He pulled her slightly closer again, making her feel his heat.

Well, if he could be hot, she would be cold. Let him think she couldn't care less about his little games.

"Serena seems nice," she said, pasting on a cool smile.

He appeared casually amused by the change in subject. "I'm enjoying her company."

"Naturally," she said somewhat sourly. No one was safe from a womanizer like Brant.

The amusement left his face and he scowled. "What does that mean?"

"What do you think it means?" Two could play at this.

"Are you going to answer all my questions with a question?" he said, the scowl still in place.

"Is that what I'm doing?"

His glance sharpened. "You thought I'd ignore her, didn't you?"

The thought had briefly crossed her mind, but she knew he would never miss an opportunity to charm a woman, whether young or old, beautiful or plain.

But she had to admit she was still annoyed with Phillip. "Actually, I know Phillip meant well, but I wish he hadn't put her in this predicament. Believe me, I know what it's like being an ugly duckling."

His head went back in shock. "You? Never!"

"It's true. I was always very plain-looking."

"You're kidding, right?"

"I'm not. Ask my father. He was very good at telling me how plain I was." She smiled grimly, remembering all the hurt. How many times had she looked into the mirror and wished she was beautiful? "Naturally he was delighted when I suddenly started to blossom into something resembling a female."

Brant's eyes probed far too deeply. "Shouldn't a father's love be unconditional?"

"Not my father," she said, on some level surprised she was telling him so much. "He only likes being with women who are beautiful."

"Women?"

She pretended not to care. "My parents are divorced. Luckily my mother settled down to a life of bliss with a man who truly loves her. Dad's on his third marriage, to a model half his age."

"How do you feel about that?"

"I'm thrilled my mother found happiness."

"And your father?"

She'd suddenly had enough. Already she'd told him more than she should have about herself.

She glanced back at the table to where the others were talking. "We were talking about Serena."

His eyes said she wasn't fooling him but he'd accept the change in subject anyway. "Serena's a nice kid."

"She wouldn't appreciate being called a kid. She's not much younger than me."

"But you're so much more—"

"Cynical?"

He broke into a sexy half smile. "I was going to say mature."

Before she could stop it, she found herself smiling back at him.

"You should smile at me more often, Kia."

As Serena had, she stumbled—just a little—then recovered. "But if I smile, you might think I like you," she said with false sweetness.

As if he realized he'd let down his guard, the smile froze on his lips. "We wouldn't want that to happen, now would we?" he said, but his voice sounded flat and he'd withdrawn into himself.

Thankfully the song ended. She cleared her throat and went to move away. "Thank you for the dance, Brant."

But he surprised her by holding on to her arm. "Say it again, Kia."

She blinked. "What?"

"Say my name again."

In a way, she was grateful the womanizer was back. "Brant Matthews," she said defiantly.

Looking satisfied, he dropped her arm the way he'd drop her heart if she dared let him near it.

Not that she would, she told herself on the way back to the table, then forced her face to maintain a calm expression when Phillip gave her an odd look. Phillip didn't know it, but he'd taken on the role of a buffer between her and the man who was her principal employer.

She spent the next hour listening to a couple of speeches, then talking to the other guests at the table and to the staff who stopped by to pay their respects to the top table.

"Hello, Phillip."

Kia blinked as a wave of apprehension swept over her. She'd seen a picture of this woman hidden in Phillip's desk. Lynette Kelly. Phillip's ex-girlfriend.

Phillip smiled coldly. "Lynette. What brings you here?"

The other woman straightened her shoulders. "I'm here with Matthew Wright," she said quietly, looking beautiful in a silky black evening gown, her dark hair framing a lovely oval face with high cheekbones and a dainty nose.

"So you've finally found your Mr. Right,

have you?" Phillip said rather nastily, and Kia turned to look at him in dismay. He and Lynette had been deeply in love until her career as a flight attendant had come between them.

Lynette's chin lifted with an odd dignity. "Yes, Phillip. I believe I have."

Kia was sure she was the only one who heard Phillip suck in a sharp breath. Thankfully the others at the table didn't appear to realize what was going on.

Except Brant, she noted.

"What a coincidence," Phillip said, recovering quickly as he picked up Kia's hand and eyed Lynette with cold triumph. "I've found the right one this time, too. Kia's agreed to marry me."

Two

"**M**a-marry?" Lynette stuttered just as there was a lull in conversation at the table. Then all hell seemed to break loose.

"Marry? Who's getting married?"

"You and Kia are getting married?"

"Oh, I just *knew* something serious was going on between you two."

Kia was frozen in her seat. It wasn't often she was lost for words, but this time she was, shock causing any protest to wedge in her throat.

Had Phillip just said what she thought he'd said? In front of everyone?

He looked at Kia, brought her hand to his lips and kissed it. "I know we were going to wait until after Christmas, darling, but I think now's as good a time as any." He smiled, but his eyes implored her not to make a scene. "Forgive me for telling everyone our little secret?"

She was going to kill him. Doing a favor for her boss was one thing, but this was going too far. But what could she do? Make him look a fool in front of everyone? In front of Lynette? The other woman had been the reason for all this pretence in the first place.

A faint thread of hysteria rose in her throat. "I—"

"Details," someone cut across her, which was probably best because she had no idea what she'd been about to say.

"Yes, give us details. We want to know everything."

"Yeah, like where's your engagement ring?"

Phillip laughed. "We don't have any details yet. I only proposed tonight." He smiled lovingly at her. "We'll pick out a ring after Christmas, won't we, darling?"

Still in shock, Kia was trying to think what to say. "Um…"

"How romantic," one of the women said on a sigh.

"Yes, isn't it," Brant said, a penetrating look in his eyes that made Kia feel as if he knew everything about them and didn't like what he saw.

Yet Phillip had been insistent when they'd started this charade that no one know about it but themselves. Not even Brant. *Especially* not Brant, Phillip had said, worried his business partner might think he was being irresponsible. Apparently Brant still hadn't forgiven Phillip for some silly error he'd made with one of their clients. It hadn't been that important, Phillip had told her, but Brant had been watching him like a hawk ever since.

And she'd gone along with the secret for her own reasons. It had afforded her some degree of protection against the desire she saw in Brant's eyes. Always he was around… watching…waiting…as if ready to pounce on her the minute Phillip was out of sight, both physically and mentally.

"You're a lucky woman, Kia," Lynette suddenly said in a quiet voice, her face pale as she took a shaky breath. An awkward silence fell. "Well, I must get back to my table." She looked at Phillip, her bleak eyes riveted on his face. "Congratulations, Phillip. Goodbye."

His very breath seemed to leave him, then he appeared to gather his resolve. "Goodbye, Lynette," he said brusquely.

She walked away with stiff dignity that made Kia inwardly flinch. God, she felt bad about her involvement in all this, having met the woman now. It had started out so inno-cently…so uncomplicated. No one should have gotten hurt.

But Lynette was hurting badly right now. And so was Phillip. He couldn't have known she'd be here. Couldn't have prepared himself for—

Suddenly something fell into place and Kia realized that Phillip *had* known Lynette was going to be here tonight. It was the reason he'd been distant after lunch. The reason he'd given her the diamond necklace to wear. And the reason he'd asked Brant to dance with her, making sure she was on the dance floor and on show for the other woman.

To *hurt* Lynette.

The thought tore at Kia's insides. She'd never deliberately hurt someone in her life and didn't appreciate being a part of this now. She'd tell Phillip on the way home and make him promise to set things right after this once and for all.

It was as well the DJ announced he would take a break while they served the meal, and everything became a flurry of people returning to their tables.

All at once she realized Brant was watching her with narrowed intensity. Every instinct inside her told her not to let him figure out the truth just yet. He was the senior partner—the boss—and he would take no hostages.

She felt uneasy as Brant continued to watch them while they worked their way through each course. By the time dessert was served she felt as though her relationship with her new fiancé had been scrutinized.

Suddenly Phillip pushed his wheelchair back from the table and gave a weak smile to the other guests. "You'll have to excuse me, but I think I'll call it a night. My leg is really starting to give me hell." He looked at Kia apologetically. "Darling, you stay and enjoy yourself."

She'd been concentrating so hard on Brant

that his announcement took her completely by surprise. Come to think of it, Phillip hadn't eaten much and he'd been very quiet through-out the meal.

Probably from guilt, she decided, anger building at him even *thinking* about leaving her here and throwing her to the wolves. Or should that be *wolf?*

As in, Brant Matthews.

"I'll come with you," she said, reaching for her purse, determined to get away from all prying eyes.

He gave her a tired smile that was offset by the wary gleam in his eyes. "There's no need, darling. I'll be going straight to bed."

Kia wasn't about to let Phillip get away with this. They needed to talk. *Tonight.*

She pushed her chair back farther. "Still, I think I'll go home, too."

Phillip put up a hand. "Please stay, darling. I don't want to spoil your fun."

What fun? She didn't call Brant's company fun, not with him watching her, waiting. And if Phillip called her "darling" one more time, she was going to scream. She was no man's "darling," not when her father liked to call her his "darling girl."

She turned back to Phillip, ready to insist on going with him. Only the look in his eyes stopped her dead. Seeing Lynette again had upset him.

Compassion stirred within her, diminishing her anger to a degree. "Okay, Phillip. I understand. You just get plenty of rest so that we can go to the art exhibition tomorrow." Her eyes said she intended talking to him then about all this.

His eyes darted away uneasily. "I'll call you in the morning."

"I'll make sure she gets home safely," Brant said out of the blue.

Kia's heart lurched. She couldn't imagine being in the confines of a car with Brant. Why, even the ballroom wasn't enough to stop his silent seduction.

"No, that's okay," she said quickly. "I'll take a taxi."

"Not in that, you won't," Brant said arrogantly, giving her breasts a raking glance in the clinging silver dress. "There was a woman attacked just last week after she left one of the hotels by herself."

"Yes, and they caught the guy, remember?" she pointed out, resisting the urge to tug at her bodice and cover her cleavage. "It was an old boyfriend." She turned to Phillip. "I'll be fine."

But Phillip was frowning. "No, Brant's right. You're too attractive to be out on your own late at night."

Okay, this was getting crazy.

"Phillip, don't be ridiculous. I'm a grown woman. I know how to take care of myself."

Phillip opened his mouth, but it was Brant who spoke. "I don't think it's ridiculous that your..." He paused. "...*fiancé* is concerned for your safety."

She grimaced inwardly. What could she say to that? "Fine. You can drive me home then."

God help her.

Satisfied with that, Phillip fobbed off someone's suggestion that they announce the engagement over the microphone before he left. She shuddered at the suggestion, knowing it would be public knowledge soon enough. Oh, heavens, and wasn't that idiotic journalist who'd written the comment about her getting her hooks into Phillip going to just love all this?

Thankfully Phillip's male nurse, Rick, was in the hotel and was ready and waiting by the time Kia pushed the wheelchair through the ballroom doors. She tried to speak to Phillip, but all she got was a quick apology and a promise to talk later.

Then Rick wheeled him away. Suddenly the hardest thing to do was turn around and walk back into that room. Brant would be there with his arrogance and his hostility, and if he said so much as one word out of place, she would pour his drink over his head.

She smiled to herself. As a matter of fact, she hoped he did, she mused as she pushed open the doors and immediately felt those hard eyes eating her up from across the room. They scorched her with a look that bordered on physical intensity.

Unable to stop herself, she glanced at Brant. Through the sea of people and smoke-filled air, her knees weakened as sexual heat enveloped her, even as he pretended to be listening to something Simon said to him.

And it *was* a pretence. Every feminine instinct told her that he'd like nothing more than to sweep her into his arms and lose himself in her body. *Her body.* She had to remember that's all he wanted.

"Hey, babe. Wanna dance?"

Startled, she turned and looked into the face of Danny Tripp, the teenage son of one of the executives who worked a few days a week in the accounts department, and who turned beetroot-red whenever she came into the room. She'd never been able to get him to say more than two words at a time.

But not tonight, it seemed. Tonight tall, young, clean-cut Danny Tripp, fortified by alcohol, had a silly grin on his face and was game for anything, especially with a group of his mates egging him on.

Great. Now she had *two* men lusting after her. Well, one was really only a boy in a man's body. And the other? Yes, Brant Matthews was all man. And more. Much more.

She glanced across the room and saw the alert look in his eyes that told her he sensed another male moving in on his territory. *His* territory. How ridiculous to think that way. Yet she couldn't shake the feeling.

Dragging her gaze away, she gave Danny a friendly smile so that he wouldn't feel embarrassed in front of his friends. "I'd love to dance with you, Danny."

"You would?" For a moment he appeared stunned. Then he grabbed her hand and dragged her out onto the dance floor.

She stumbled into his arms when he spun around to face her, and before she knew it, he'd slid his hands onto her hips, pulled her close to his lanky body and buried his face in her hair. There was none of the finesse Brant had exhibited earlier when he'd taken her in his arms. This was pure adolescent male, hungry for sex, and all the better with a woman he fancied.

Slightly alarmed—and hearing his pals' whistles over the slow music—she put her hands against his chest and forced some distance between them. "Danny, I—"

"Don't talk, babe." He went to pull her back into position.

She held firm against him. "Dan-ny…" The tone of her voice must have gotten through to him, because the hold on her hips slackened. She breathed a sigh of relief and looked up at him, pleased to see some of the alcoholic glaze disappear from his eyes.

He gave her a self-conscious grin. "Sorry, Kia. I guess you went to my head."

She relaxed with a smile, finding his boyishness easier to handle. "I think the drink had more to do with it than me."

He shrugged wryly. "Yeah, well, I'm not used to drinking rum."

Kia suspected he wasn't used to drinking at all. "I once got drunk on brandy and was sick for a full week."

"*You* got drunk? No foolin'?"

"I was young once, too, you know," she joked, even while her heart cramped with pain at the reason she'd been drinking. It had been the day her father had married his second wife.

He hadn't wanted his "plain-looking" daughter at the wedding—or that's what he'd been telling her mother when Kia had accidentally picked up the telephone to make a call.

She'd been crushed by his rejection, though at fifteen she should have been used to his insensitivity. Afterward she'd feigned ignorance when her mother had gently explained about her father's remarriage. She had then gone out and gotten rotten drunk at a friend's party, learning the hard way that drinking didn't solve a thing.

"I hope you won't spread that around?" she said now, pushing aside her painful memories to smile up at Danny.

"Er…" His eyes darted to his friends at the table behind them, then back to her. "Sorry. What did you say?"

Someone yelled out, "Yea, Danny," but she pretended not to notice. They were only having fun. "I said I hope you won't tell anyone that

I once got drunk. I have a reputation to uphold," she teased.

His gaze went beyond her again, seemed to hesitate. Then, taking a deep breath, he pulled her up close once more. "I won't say anything," he said as if whispering sweet nothings in her ear. "I promise, babe."

He was obviously more concerned with his own reputation than hers, so it was silly to feel a flutter of apprehension just because he wanted to show off for his friends. He was really just a kid who'd had too much to drink.

Should she wait until the music stopped, then go back to her table? Or go now? The room was full of people. Surely nothing would happen to her in the middle of the dance floor....

She jumped when he began to nuzzle her neck. Okay, no way could she let this go any further. "Danny, I—"

"Let the lady go," a deep male voice said

beside them, startling them both, the warning in Brant's voice clearly evident.

Danny shoved himself away from Kia, a slightly belligerent look on his face until he caught sight of who'd spoken. His cheeks began to turn red as he looked at Brant's thunderous expression. "I'm sorry, Mr. Matthews," he said quickly. "I wasn't doing anything wrong."

"I know exactly what you were doing, Daniel." Brant jerked his head at the table behind them. "I suggest you go back to your table before I decide to tell Mr. Reid what you were trying to do with his PA."

Danny looked horrified. "I was just fooling around, Mr. Matthews—promise," he said, then scurried away, obviously terrified he would lose his job.

Kia couldn't help but feel sorry for the young man. Brant could be a formidable figure when he chose to be, though why he chose to throw his weight around now was anybody's guess.

She winced inwardly. That wasn't quite true. She knew *exactly* why he wanted Danny away from her. But before she could think further, Brant swept her into his arms and began to lead her around the dance floor. His touch was impersonal enough, so why did she feel acutely aware of him and his sexual power over her?

Angry with herself for her reaction, she shot him a look that would make a lesser man stumble. "You didn't need to frighten him like that."

"Yes, I did."

And she saw that deep down he did. It fit his dangerous persona. The predator who never gave up his prey without a fight. All very subliminal, yet it was there, hidden beneath his civilized exterior. God, was she the only one who saw it? Who felt it? She must be.

She swallowed a lump of apprehension. "You had no right to interfere."

His grip tightened. "I had every right. Philip would expect me to protect his…fiancée."

She ignored another insulting pause. "Danny's just a boy. He was having some fun, that's all."

A cynical smile immediately twisted his lips. "He's a young man who was almost having his way with you right there on the floor." He shrugged. "But, hey, if that's how you get your kicks, then maybe—"

"Shut up, Brant."

For a moment it was hard to tell who was the more surprised, but then a satisfied light came into his blue eyes. "Hurrah! She said my name."

Kia found herself exchanging a subtle look of amusement with him. Okay, so he'd won that small victory. She could allow him that, seeing he really had saved her from a possibly unpleasant situation.

"If it'll make you feel any better, I'll talk to Danny on Monday," he said. "For now, it'll do him good to stew over the weekend. He needs to learn a lesson about not making a move on the boss's woman."

Which boss? she wanted to ask, a tingle running down her spine at the thought of being Brant's woman. She grimaced. *One* of Brant's women. "Thank you."

There was a moment's pause, then, "So congratulations are in order," he said in a harsh voice that suddenly matched his eyes.

Unable to bring herself to say yes, she merely nodded.

"I'm surprised," he continued. "Most women couldn't have kept it a secret."

"I'm not most women."

"True." But it didn't sound like a compliment. His burning gaze slid down the column of her throat, to the necklace, and rested there for a moment. "Diamonds look good on you," he said almost as if he disliked her for it. "Another expensive gift from Phillip?"

"Another?"

"As well as the Porsche."

Good grief. Did he think Phillip had bought the car for her? She felt her cheeks redden. "Phillip did *not* give me the Porsche."

His eyes flickered with surprise. "But he gave you the necklace, right?" His expression darkened, grew stormy. "He's generous to a fault."

The way he said it was as if Phillip was generous and *she* was at fault. For a moment she wondered what she'd ever done to this man— apart from *not* hopping into bed with him.

As for the necklace, how could she tell him she was giving it back to Phillip? He'd have to ask why. So let him think what he liked. He did anyway.

After that, he seemed to sense her withdrawal, because he remained quiet while they danced around the floor. Kia fought hard to concentrate on being angry with him, but the music was growing insistent, bringing his body against her own, each step sensuously rubbing leg against leg.

His hand rested on her hip, every movement making his palm slide a little up, a little down.

Up. Down.

Hot. Cool.

In. Out.

Oh, God.

"Are you all right?"

His husky words snapped Kia's head back and she gazed into eyes that smoldered with awareness. Her heart lurched sideways, his magnetism so potent, so compelling that she could imagine him taking her right here and now in a raw act of possession that had everything to do with pure sex and erotic pleasure and nothing to do with reason. And he knew. Oh, yes, he knew, because that feeling was rushing through him, too. She could see it in his eyes. In every beat of his heart.

"It's—" she moistened her lips "—a bit hot

in here, that's all," she said, pretending it was the crowd of people on the dance floor affecting her, and not him. "Too many people wanting to let their hair down, I guess."

His gaze dropped to her mouth, and the blue of his eyes darkened. Then he glanced up at the blond hair she'd put up for tonight. "Do *you* ever let your hair down, Kia?" he murmured.

What was he really asking? Whether she'd dare go to bed with him? Somehow, somewhere, she had to find the strength to pull herself out of this. If Phillip were here…

Of course!

Stronger now, she planted a cool smile on her lips. "Phillip's really the only one I let my hair down for now."

He tensed, a muscle ticking at his jaw. "Phillip didn't seem himself tonight."

She knew what he was implying. That Lynette's presence had upset him. "He's been doing too much this week."

"Nothing else?"

Kia remembered the deciphering way Brant had looked at her and Phillip after Lynette had left and she felt a flutter of panic. "Maybe being the center of attention tonight was too much for him."

"Perhaps."

Everything had been crazy since the accident, and with Phillip having been told he'd have a permanent limp, she knew Brant couldn't be sure that *hadn't* been the problem tonight. She was banking on that to save her from further interrogation.

The music ended, and her heart skipped with relief when he let her slip from his arms without another word. He escorted her back to the table, fortunately without touching her, but she still resisted the urge to fan herself as she took her seat. One more dance with him and she'd have gone up in smoke.

"Are you enjoying yourself?" Serena asked.

Kia smiled at the other woman and tried not to show how her pulse was bubbling like the fresh glass of champagne in her hand. What a question. How could she enjoy herself when every look sent her way told her that this woman's date wanted her with a passion.

"I'm having a great time," she lied, watching Brant sit down on the opposite side of Serena. "I just wish Phillip hadn't left so early." That, at least, was the truth.

Serena's eyes turned sympathetic. "He needs time to adjust."

Kia felt her throat close up. She didn't deserve Serena's sympathy. Or anyone else's, for that matter. She was such a fraud. "I know," was all she could manage.

After that, talk around the table turned to other things. Her heart took the chance to settle back to its regular beat as she listened to the discussions going on around her. They were all such nice people.

She glanced at Brant, his dark head tilted toward Serena while she spoke to him. Well, *nearly* all of them were nice. She couldn't exactly call Brant Matthews "nice."

It didn't apply to a man with probing eyes and an inscrutable expression, a man whose body coiled with barely controlled sensuality but bordered on an unfriendliness that belonged to an archenemy.

Thankfully the music started up again, this time playing rock and roll, and Simon asked her to dance. Desperate to forget thoughts of Brant, who was now asking Serena to dance with him, she willingly went with the older man to the dance floor, where he showed her that being middle-aged still made him capable of some daring moves.

"He'll be paying for that tomorrow," his wife teased to Kia when she returned to the table with Simon after only one song.

Kia smiled, but before she could catch her

breath, Bill Stewart grabbed her hand and insisted on a dance, too. She figured out then that they were making sure she was having a good time even without her fiancé.

When she eventually got to sit down, she saw Simon about to get to his feet again. "No more," she gasped, reaching for the jug of ice water. They were killing her with kindness.

"Oh, but—" Simon began.

"No more," Brant said firmly across the table, the look in his eyes reminding them all who was boss. "Kia looks tired."

Kia didn't want to agree with him, but she didn't want to dance again either. "I am a little," she smilingly apologized to Simon.

"That's okay," the older man said with obvious relief. "I wasn't sure I had another one in me anyway."

After that, the music got even louder, until it became more impossible to talk. It wasn't long before the older couples decided to call it a night.

"Would you ladies like to go home soon?" Brant said, encompassing both her and Serena with his question. "It's nearly midnight."

Rather than going home with Brant, Kia would have sat here all night if she knew she hadn't been inconveniencing Serena. "That's up to both of you."

"I'm ready when you are," Serena agreed, giving a delicate yawn followed by a self-conscious laugh. "I have an early appointment in the morning anyway."

"No sleep-in for you then," Kia teased.

Brant quickly finished off his drink. "Right. Let's go," he rasped, getting to his feet.

Startled by his tone, Kia got to her feet, too, followed by Serena, who didn't seem to notice and continued to talk while they made their way through the tables to the exit.

Kia listened even while she wondered why Brant's face looked like thunder. Had it been her mention of sleeping in tomorrow morning?

Did it remind him of being in bed? Of making love? She must have reminded him that he *wasn't* about to get any sex tonight. Not from Serena. And certainly not from *her.*

Of course, he would still have plenty of other woman friends who would willingly sacrifice themselves for his pleasure. He only had to make a phone call and it would be his.

But she soon forgot all that when they reached the front of the hotel and were discussing where they lived while waiting for Brant's car to be brought around. It appeared Serena lived closest.

"Then we'll drop you off first, if you don't mind," Brant said as the gray Mercedes glided to a stop in front of them.

Serena smiled shyly. "Of course I don't mind," she said, and before Kia could do a thing about it, Brant was holding the back door open for Serena and she had slid onto the backseat.

Kia was tempted to slide in right next to her,

but as if he knew, Brant took her by the elbow and walked her to the front passenger door.

His touch made her shiver in the balmy night air. Soon she'd be alone with a man who had no need to touch to get his way. A man who had perfected foreplay with just a look. Perhaps it was as well she was an "engaged" woman now.

Three

Kia consoled herself on the way home that at least her presence wouldn't give Brant the opportunity to seduce the innocent Serena. Not that she really thought he would now, not after the brotherly way he'd been treating the younger woman all night.

Then she remembered her father and all the young women who'd passed through his life and she knew that some men just couldn't help themselves.

Five minutes later, she watched from the car while Brant walked Serena to the front door of her house. The security light had come on at their approach and Kia saw everything clearly. She breathed a sigh of relief when Brant gave Serena a smile and a quick peck on the cheek, then strode back to the car.

"Was that chaste enough for you?" he mocked as he started the engine.

Chaste? A kiss from this man could never be considered chaste. Not for her, anyway.

She forced a cool smile. "I didn't think you knew what the word meant."

He smiled grimly as he pulled out from the curb. "I could say the same about you."

"Me?"

He glanced sideways, his eyes boldly raking over her. "Sweetheart, you *ooze* sex appeal. Why do you think young Danny was falling over himself?" Obviously seeing her surprise, his eyes narrowed. "Surely Phillip's told you how sexy you are?"

Sexy? No, Phillip had never told her that.

"Yes, of course," she lied.

"You don't sound too sure."

She stiffened. "Of course I'm sure. It's just that…" *Think.* "Well, since the accident we've been concentrating on him rather than me."

He appeared to consider that. "He's going through a tough time right now." Once more his gaze slid over her, almost contemptuously this time. "But if any woman can make him think like a man again, it's you."

She didn't appreciate the comment. "You've missed your calling. You should be doing talk shows."

This time he laughed. A deep, rich sound that made her catch her breath and confirmed why women of all kinds wanted him. She didn't even *like* him and *this* was her reaction.

Luckily for her, they came to some night roadwork and Brant had to slow the car and concentrate for the next kilometer. After that, except for her directing him, they both remained quiet until they reached her street.

"It's the house at the end," she said as they came around the corner into the leafy cul-de-sac.

A few moments later he pulled into the driveway and cut the engine. "You live here by yourself?" he asked, his eyes going over the ground-level house nestled amongst the lush garden. It was obviously too big for one person.

"I live by myself, yes, but the house has been divided into two. The owner lives in one apartment and I live in the other."

It was a bonus that June didn't drive, so Kia got to use the garage at the far end of the driveway. But why, oh, why hadn't she driven herself tonight? If she'd known Phillip would leave early and she'd be stranded with Brant, she would have insisted on taking her Porsche.

The Porsche Brant thought Phillip had bought for her.

He opened his door, letting in the late-night sounds of a tropical summer. "I'll walk you inside."

She'd known he would. Her front door was actually around the back of the house, so it wouldn't be possible to dismiss him easily. The minute he saw her walking down the driveway alongside the house he'd be out of the car and following her anyway.

"It's around the back." She moved to get out of the car, but her long dress proved difficult, and before she knew it he stood beside her, offering her his hand. For a moment she hesitated. Already her pulse was skittering all over the place. What would his touch do to her?

Having no option but to appear unruffled, she held her breath and put her hand on his. Her skin immediately tingled from the contact, but surprisingly his fingers didn't close around hers. His hand remained open, palm up, allowing her to grip him as she chose.

Is this how he lets a woman make love to him? At her own pace?

That thought spread the tingle through her body as her fingers closed around his hand and she pressed her palm against his, using his strength to bring her to her feet.

He stepped back before their bodies could touch further, making her grateful for small mercies.

"It's this way," she said huskily and hurried forward, the path illuminated by small garden lights mingling through the palm trees, the clicking of her high heels in competition with a chorus of green tree frogs.

But when she came up to the door, it was standing open. She began to frown, then gave a soft gasp as realization hit. Someone had broken in.

"Oh, my God," she whispered in disbelief.

"Stay there." Brant strode the few feet to the

door, swearing softly when he tread on some broken glass. He reached inside for the nearest switch, flooding the kitchen with light.

Kia came up behind him and they both stood there looking around. At first it appeared as if nothing had happened but the glass on the floor showed that someone had smashed one of the panels on the door.

"Careful," Brant warned, stepping over the mess, then helping her while she lifted the skirt of her long dress with one hand and gingerly stepped over the glass.

Kia's heart was almost jumping out of her chest. "Do you think he's still here?" she whispered.

Brant peered toward the darkened hallway, his expression hard. "If he is…" He pulled his cell phone out of his jacket pocket. "He's going to regret it."

Kia shivered as he dialed the police and spoke quietly for a moment. She almost felt sorry for the robber if he was still here. He'd be in for a shock if Brant got hold of him.

He swore as he ended the call. "They've had a busy night. They could be a while."

Kia's stomach churned with anxiety. She'd hate to think what would happen if she were here alone. For the first time, she was glad of Brant's presence. "What now?"

He reached over to grab a knife from the block on the sink. "I guess I'm going to play the bloody hero," he muttered, stepping toward the hallway, but he stopped when he saw her face. "What's the matter?"

"You're not going to use that, are you?"

He grimaced. "It's only for protection. Come on. Stick with me."

Kia needed no second bidding. She stuck like wallpaper while they went from room to room, switching on each light, her knees knocking with relief when no one jumped out at them.

In the loungeroom they discovered her laptop and DVD player missing, plus a small antique clock, along with other knickknacks. Her bedroom appeared untouched, thank God. She'd hate to think of some stranger handling her personal things. Perhaps fondling her silky bra and panties…

She shuddered, and Brant put his hand on her forearm and turned her to face him. "Are you all right?"

"Yes," she murmured, though she knew she wasn't. She couldn't seem to stop shaking.

"Shhh," he said, starting to massage her arm in a comforting gesture that made her drop her gaze to his hand on her, suddenly wanting to lean into him and let his strength wrap around her.

She looked up and all at once he was staring into her eyes.

"Kia?" he growled, and she opened her lips slightly despite a silken thread of warning in his voice. He was going to kiss her…. She wanted him to, dear God, she did.

Just then the sound of crunching glass came from the kitchen and a male voice called out, "This is the police. Everything all right in there?"

Brant immediately stepped back. "About bloody time," he rasped without looking at her and left her side to stride down the hallway. "We're here, Constable," he said more loudly. "We were just seeing if there was any damage."

Kia stood there for a moment, fighting intense disappointment. Brant obviously hadn't suffered from the same frustration—or if he had, he hadn't shown it. He'd turned away from her so fast she'd almost got whiplash watching him.

Which only reminded her that's exactly what he'd do if he ever got her into bed. He'd use her, then he'd walk away without a second glance.

Kia took a deep breath and straightened her shoulders. Now she felt strong again. She'd resisted him this far and would continue to do so. She'd been weakened by the shock of the robbery, that's all.

For the next ten minutes she sat at the kitchen table and answered questions for the two very nice policemen who'd responded to the call, while Brant leaned back against the sink and watched the proceedings like a judge in a courtroom. He certainly made the younger policeman uneasy, by the looks of things, though the older one didn't bat an eyelid.

"Probably an addict," the older policeman said now, giving a world-weary shrug. "Got to get their fix somehow. Just as well you were wearing that necklace, Miss Benton, and didn't leave it at home."

Kia gave a soft gasp as her hand went to the diamonds circling her neck. Then she saw Brant's jaw clench and the way his eyes burned her and she couldn't help but think he was somehow angry over Phillip giving her the necklace.

The policeman interrupted her thoughts by going on to suggest ways of tightening her security, including putting a bolt on the door and getting a dog.

"Oh, but we do have a dog. I mean, the lady in the apartment next door has a dog." Something occurred to her. "Oh, no. I wonder if he broke into June's place, as well? The house has been divided in two, you see." She swallowed. "Do you think you could check? She's not home this weekend, thank goodness. She went to visit her sister and took Ralphie with her."

"I'll go take a look around," the younger policeman said after getting a nod from his boss, then nervously looked at Brant before leaving the room, as if glad to get out from under such a strong presence.

The older policeman glanced at Kia. "Have you got someone to stay with you tonight,

Miss Benton? Something like this can shake people up pretty bad."

"*I'll* be staying with her," Brant said before she could open her mouth.

She shot to her feet. She couldn't have Brant stay here. She just couldn't. "I can look after myself. I don't need anyone. I—"

"What if he comes back?" Brant cut across her.

The spew of words froze on her lips. Somehow she managed a short laugh. "He won't. He got what he wanted."

"Did he?"

She shivered and hugged her bare arms. "Stop it. You're scaring me."

"Well, you should be bloody scared," he said, straightening away from the sink. "You've got a door with a broken lock and no one close enough to hear you scream." His jaw tautened, making him look dark and dangerous. "I'm staying."

How silly to feel relief. She should be more scared of Brant and her own attraction for him than of being robbed again. Only if the robber came back he might not only want to rob her. He might want more than that….

"I really think that's a good idea, Miss Benton," the older policeman coaxed, looking at her in a fatherly fashion, reminding her that they weren't alone.

She swallowed deeply. "Yes, of course."

Right then the younger policeman stepped back into the kitchen, interrupting them. "Everything's fine next door." He shot a look at his boss. "Sarge, that call we were expecting just came through."

"Right." The older man straightened and immediately put his notebook in his pocket. "We'll be in touch," he told them quickly, then was gone.

A moment's tense silence stretched between her and Brant, then she cleared her throat, determined to be as businesslike as possible. "I'll get the couch ready for you."

Brant's mouth twisted. "I doubt I'll get much sleep on that two-seater in your loungeroom."

She felt as if her breath cut out. *Was he asking to share her bed?* Over her dead body.

Well, maybe not her *dead* body, she mused, hurrying to the refrigerator to get a cool drink. "Isn't that the point? To stay awake and protect me?" She lifted out the jug of cold water, almost tempted to hold it up to her forehead to cool herself down. "Anyway, it opens out to a sofa bed. You'll have plenty of room."

He began loosening his tie. "Fine. I like being able to spread out."

"That must be a novelty for you," she said before she could stop herself.

The look in his eyes held a spark of eroticism. "You make it sound like there's a woman in my bed every day."

She feigned ignorance. "You mean there isn't?"

"Sweetheart, I'm not married. I only let a woman in my bed when I'm looking for some affection."

"That's what I said. Every day." She placed the jug on the bench and walked toward the hallway door. "I'll get you a blanket," she said before he could respond. She had to get out of that room or she'd strangle him with her bare hands. Either that or smother him with one of the pillows she was about to get him.

The ringing of the telephone next to him woke Brant with a start the next morning. It seemed as if he'd only just fallen asleep, having tossed and turned for most of the night, blaming the sofa but knowing it was because the sexiest woman alive lay in a bed not meters away from him, with only a thin wall between them.

So he didn't appreciate being woken now. "Yes?" he barked into the mouthpiece.

A moment's silence, then a man's shocked voice came down the line. "Brant!"

Brant's eyes flew open. "Phil?"

The other man sucked in a sharp breath. "What the hell? Where's Kia?"

"Look, it's not what you think," Brant growled, shooting to a sitting position and regaining his composure. "Someone broke into her place last night. I slept on the sofa so I could keep an eye on her, that's all."

"Is she okay?" Phil asked, anxious now.

"She was a bit shook up last night, but I'm sure she'll be fine in the light of day."

He looked up and saw Kia standing in the doorway. Her blue eyes were sleepy, her blond hair sexily tousled, not a bit of makeup on her beautiful face as she wrapped the sash of a silky blue creation around her waist. She looked so bloody gorgeous he had to stop himself from throwing the phone down and ravishing her on the spot.

"I'm glad you were there for her," Phil said slowly, dragging Brant's thoughts away from the woman in front of him. Phil still sounded depressed.

"Phil, I'm sure she would rather have had you here," he said, watching her eyes come fully awake at the mention of the other man's name.

"Is that Phillip?" she said, stepping into the room and hurrying toward him. In an instant Brant could feel her female heat coiling around him. Could hear the silky swish of her thighs. The soft gasps of her breath that came closer and closer. If he reached out, he might just be able to caress her.

Instead he held out the phone. "Yeah, it's Phil."

She snatched it to her and immediately turned her back on him. "Phillip? Did Brant explain what happened?" She gave a delicate shudder. "It was awful. I can't believe someone would do this." She listened for a moment, then said, "He broke the glass door. The police think…"

She continued to talk, but Brant had stopped listening. And he'd almost stopped breathing. She didn't know it, but with the morning sun streaming in the room he could see straight through her gossamer robe to the line of her buttocks. God, how he'd love to run his hands over them. They'd be so smooth to his touch.

Giving a silent groan, he leaned his head back against the pillows and closed his eyes. Dammit, he had to stop this. She wasn't worth the looking…the wanting….

"Brant?"

Did she have to say his name in such a husky voice? As if she was his lover, waiting for him to stir. The next thing she'd be reaching out to touch him….

"Yes?" His voice sounded rough, like the night he'd just had.

"Are you awake?"

"No. I always talk in my sleep," he mocked and opened his eyes. Disappointment rippled through him when he saw she'd moved out of the sunlight.

Her mouth tightened. "That's one thing *I'll* never find out."

"No, you won't, will you?" And suddenly it was the biggest regret of his life. His lips twisted. Okay, that and getting involved with Julia all those years ago. She hadn't been too innocent when she'd run off and married his brother.

He threw back the sheet and swung his legs over the side of the sofa bed, his black briefs his only covering. "Tell me. Does Phillip ever talk in his sleep?" he asked, forcing himself to remember who this woman belonged to…and what she was about.

Money.

She gave a light laugh. "Only to murmur sweet nothings in my ear."

An intense jealousy slashed through him. It should have been *him* who whispered in her ear. *Him* who lay beside her. *Him* who made love to her. That's what felt right. Not her and Phillip. Every minute he grew more certain of it.

He reached for his trousers. God, what was going on here? Why didn't he suddenly feel right about those two? There was something he couldn't quite put his finger on. Something important. Yet all he had was a gut feeling he couldn't shake. And a bloody hunger for Kia Benton that wouldn't stop.

"Would you like coffee before you go?"

At the crack in her voice he looked up and caught her appraising his bare chest and taut stomach. Despite being newly engaged, the look in her eye said she wanted *him*.

His muscles immediately tensed as he zipped up and asked the question that hit him from out of nowhere. "How come you didn't call Phillip last night?" All at once he found it interesting that she hadn't gone running to her fiancé after the burglary.

She'd been about to turn away, but now her eyelids flickered, as if the question startled her. "What? Er...I didn't want to worry him."

"If you were my fiancée, I'd *want* you to worry me."

She moistened those oh-so-enticing lips. "You know he was tired and in pain when he left the party."

"I'd still want to know if you were in danger."

Her chin angled. "Phillip's not like you, Brant."

No, he wasn't, was he? Phillip was a one-woman man. And that woman was Lynette Kelly, of that Brant was suddenly certain. Ever since he'd seen Phillip's reaction to his old girlfriend at the Christmas party last night, he'd had this deep nagging feeling. And what about Lynette's reaction to Phillip? They were both still in love with each other, no doubt about it.

Brant looked at Kia and wondered if she knew. Surely she'd noticed something amiss?

"Forget the coffee," he rasped as he quickly slipped on his shirt and made a grab for his jacket. He had to get out of here before he did or said something he'd regret. Phillip may be in love with Lynette, but the other man obviously wasn't prepared to do anything about it. And Kia must be thanking her lucky stars she'd found a man who didn't give a damn that he was being taken to the cleaners.

Ignoring the tight knot forming in his stomach, he sat down again and began putting on his socks and shoes. "I'll call a locksmith and get him to fix the door for you." What he should really do is get someone to lock *her* up. Only then would men be safe from her beauty and self-seeking ways.

"I'm quite capable of picking up a phone."

"I didn't say you weren't, but I can get it fixed faster. I have connections."

"What you mean is you'll offer him more money to fix it today?"

"The company can afford it."

She drew in a sharp breath. "Don't be ridiculous. I won't be letting the company pay for anything."

His mouth clamped into a thin line. Who was she trying to fool? This was a token protest at best.

"So you're going to sleep another night with your door wide-open?" He stood up, ready to leave. "I could always come back and use your sofa again." It was a foolhardy threat. He'd never be able to handle another night without touching her. And he had better things to do with his time.

"I'll go to a motel."

His teeth clenched. "Fine and dandy. And when you get home, the rest of your stuff will have been stolen." Without waiting for a response, he started toward the door. "Someone will be round within the hour."

"Brant—" she warned, only to have the ring of the telephone interrupt her.

"Answer that," he said and left the house before she could get another word in. What he found interesting was that she hadn't mentioned staying at Phillip's place, when that would be the ideal solution. Perhaps she was holding out for a white wedding, he mused cynically.

Four

Later that day, when Phillip's attendant knocked on her door to pick her up to take her to the art exhibition, Kia had to take a calming breath before answering. She was furious with Brant over the locksmith he'd sent here. All the names she'd been calling him seemed too tame for the thoughts bubbling in her brain right now.

But instead of showing her feelings, she smoothed her hands down the front of her slim-fitting sleeveless dress and reached for the door handle. She wouldn't let Brant spoil her afternoon. She'd rather eat rat poison.

"G'day, Kia."

The breath caught in her throat. The man on the other side of the doorway emitted a sex appeal so potent it cracked through the air like a whip, invisibly wrapping around her body and almost pulling her toward him. Black trousers fitted his lower torso to perfection, a light gray polo shirt molded over his chest. He looked casual and confident. A man any woman would be proud to be seen with.

Anyone but her.

"Aren't you going to invite me in?" Brant said, stepping past her into the house without waiting for an invitation.

She spun around to face him. Of all the arrogant… "How dare you!" she managed to say.

He merely looked amused. "How dare I be

in your house? You didn't mind me being here last night."

She glared at him. He made it sound as if they'd been making love all night. "I'm talking about the security alarm."

His forehead creased. "He didn't do a good job?"

"Yes, he did a good job, but that's not the point. He was supposed to fix the lock, not put in an alarm system." She'd thought the man had been merely checking security risks when he'd started going from room to room. By the time she'd realized he was doing the whole thing, he'd climbed on the roof and had half the place wired.

"I thought an alarm system would be better."

"*You* thought? Where do you get off ordering an alarm for *me*?"

"I told you. The company will pay for it."

"It's not the money," she said through gritted teeth.

His eyebrows lifted with cynicism. "Really? Then what's the problem?"

"This is *my* home, Brant. *My* private life. You're interfering in it. You've no right to even be here, let alone tell someone to install an expensive piece of equipment like this. Heck, it's not even technically my house."

His shrug belied the hard gleam in his eyes. "Don't make a big deal out of this, Kia. You're Phillip's fiancée now. He wants you to be safe."

She tried not to wince. "Phillip knows about the alarm?"

"As you're now his fiancée, I suggested it and he agreed. We all know it's quite common for criminals to return to the scene of the crime. You either had to get an alarm or move."

She flashed him a look of disdain. "Oh, really. And where would you like me to live?"

"How about with your fiancé?"

She gulped and quickly spun away to turn off

the air-conditioning. Anything not to look at Brant. "Phillip and I haven't discussed that yet."

"That's what Phil said."

Relief rushed through her. "There you are then." She remembered the security alarm and glared at him. "Anyway, you and Phillip have no right to tell me what to do or what to put in my own house. And as soon as he gets here, I'll be making that quite clear."

"Then you're going to have a bit of a wait," he said, his gaze seeming to watch her reaction. "He's not coming. He rang and asked me to take you to the exhibition instead. He said he wasn't feeling up to it today."

Her stomach knotted. She didn't want to go to the exhibition with Brant. Damn Phillip for being selfish enough not to turn up. She was beginning to think taking the easy way out was a weakness he couldn't control.

"Why didn't he phone me himself?"

"He said he'd tried a couple of times but kept getting the busy signal."

She bristled with indignation. "Because the alarm was being connected to the phone line, that's why." She waved a dismissive hand. "Oh, it doesn't matter. I'm not going without Phillip."

His eyes narrowed. "Phil said one of our clients invited him to the exhibition."

"Er…yes…" She licked her lips. "But it just wouldn't be the same without Phillip. I'm sure they'll understand."

"*They* may, but *I* won't. This is a work assignment, Kia. Think of it as payment for the security alarm."

Her mouth tightened. So there *was* a catch to his free and easy statement of "the company will pay for it."

"Perhaps I should go by myself…on behalf of the company, that is. There's no need for you to waste your Saturday afternoon." She didn't want to deprive some poor besotted female of his company either.

"I wouldn't think of it as a waste. I'd like to see the exhibition, too. Early Australian art fascinates me."

It fascinated her, too, but she didn't want to say so. Yet could she spend hours with him and survive the draw of his attraction? She swallowed. It looked as though she wasn't getting a choice. But after she put in an appearance for their client, she'd make sure it was the quickest walk around the gallery on record.

An hour later she and Brant strolled through the art gallery by themselves after they'd shared an afternoon tea of pineapple scones, finger sandwiches and a delicious tropical fruit platter. Brant had been his charming self with their client and the others. A couple of times she'd even let her guard down and surprised herself by actually laughing at some of his witty remarks.

Of course, being witty and a womanizer was what he was about. That's how men like him got women into bed, and if the looks some of the other women were giving him were anything to go by, he'd have had plenty of offers today if she hadn't been around. Yes, he knew exactly how to charm the panties right off a woman. She stiffened. *Not this woman.*

"I like this painting of the early settlers," he said now, his deep voice bringing her out of her thoughts. "I saw a print of it years ago, but the brushstrokes and paint textures are nothing compared to the original." He turned to look at her. "It's very evocative, don't you agree?"

She fumbled for words when she saw the piece of work he was referring to. "Um…yes."

He arched a brow. "You sound surprised?"

A thrill raced through her, but she managed to shrug as if it were no big deal. "It's my favorite painting."

"And you didn't expect us to have the same

tastes, right?" He paused, his blue eyes darkening. "I think we'd have a lot in common if we looked closely."

She moistened suddenly dry lips. "Yes. Phillip, for one thing."

He gave a slightly bitter smile. "Ah, Phillip. We'll always have him in common, won't we?" He turned back to the painting. "Tell me. Why is this your favorite?"

Obviously he wanted to keep things on an even keel, and she was only too happy to oblige. Yet she couldn't help but feel a burst of excitement that he found the imagery of the painting as touching as she did. Perhaps there was more to him than met the eye.

She turned to the painting and let her gaze wander over the picture of their pioneer ancestors, losing herself in its sheer vibrancy and color. "I'd say it's because it personifies the Outback spirit. That it's possible to overcome any obstacle, no matter how big or daunting."

"So you like challenges?" he pounced.

She drew in a shaky breath. Always the predator. He just couldn't help himself. "*Some* challenges," she admitted.

"I like certain challenges, too," he drawled, his eyes intense. "If somebody tells me I can't have something, then that's when I want it."

And he wanted her. He had no need to say it out loud. The wanting poured from him like a familiar scent.

She plastered a smile on her lips. "Then you'd better get used to disappointment," she quipped, knowing her first instincts about him were correct. She hadn't misjudged him. Not in the slightest.

A few hours later the two of them sat at an outdoor café not far from the exhibition, sipping at fruit daiquiris. The pre-Christmas festivities were still continuing, and people were out in force and in holiday mode, enjoying a stroll along the sail-shaded Smith Street Mall, listening to a busker play her guitar, watching a mime artist perform.

Brant couldn't have cared less where they were or who was nearby. His concentration was solely and fully on one person. Kia looked as beautiful as always, with her blond hair pulled back in a French knot, and wearing a lemon-colored dress that displayed the elegant line of her neck and showed off her tanned shoulders and arms.

But something else about her today set his pulse spinning like a top. Watching her talk to the others at the gallery, he'd glimpsed an innocence in her lovely eyes that had been at odds with the knowing look in them, as if she couldn't quite hide the sweet beneath the spice. Yet *sweet* was hardly a word he'd expect to use about Kia Benton.

He swallowed some of his drink, then decided he didn't need any more intoxication right now. Apart from a brief time last night and again this morning, he'd never really been alone with her like this before. It had gone to his head—no, his *body*. His state of constant arousal was killing him.

And she knew it. That's why she wasn't quite facing him as she sat sipping her daiquiri, her body turned slightly toward the crowd.

But she was only fooling herself. There could be a brick wall between them and the attraction would still seep through. Didn't she know there was no stopping it? Not unless they made love and got it out of their systems, and then he had the feeling it would probably only intensify.

"Tell me more about your father," he said, suddenly interested in what made her tick.

She raised a wry eyebrow. "Why?"

He gave a smile. "Are you this suspicious of everyone or is it just me?"

"Just you," she said, her lips curving into a

sexy smile that was as unexpected as was her words. God. She was lovely, with her smooth cheekbones, perfect nose, eyes that could dazzle a man with just one look and a deliciously tempting mouth.

She put her glass down, and when she looked up again her face had sobered. "There's nothing much to tell. My father thinks he's one of the beautiful people. He can't stand being around someone who isn't."

Brant frowned. "You're still his daughter."

Her slim shoulders tensed. "The only reason he wants me around is because he thinks it's good for his image."

All at once something occurred to him. "Good Lord. Your father isn't Lloyd Benton, is he?"

If it were possible, she tensed even more. "The one and only."

Now he knew where she was coming from. Lloyd Benton owned the biggest fleet of used-car yards up and down the east coast of Australia. He was constantly in the newspapers with some young thing hanging off his arm— usually his current wife but not always. The man gave *sleaze* an added dimension.

"*He's* your father?"

She raised her chin in the air. "I won't apologize for him."

"I don't expect you to."

No wonder she didn't seem to hold men in high regard. Well, *some* men. He freely admitted that men like himself, who took one look and wanted to take her to bed, would only confirm her low opinion of the male species. Dammit, suddenly he was seeing another side to this woman that he wasn't sure he wanted to see.

"It certainly explains a lot about you and Phillip."

She tensed. "If you mean I want to marry someone who doesn't have to bed every beautiful woman he meets, then you're dead right.

Phillip's a nice man." Her gaze dropped to her glass, then up again. "He'll be a wonderful father and a faithful husband."

"You didn't say you loved him." And he found that interesting. *Very* interesting.

"That goes without saying."

"Does it?"

"Yes."

And perhaps it was all an act. Perhaps working on people for sympathy was how she wormed her way into men's beds…and their hearts. Perhaps it was all about paying back her father for being so weak.

"What about you?" she said, catching him off guard. "Are your parents still alive, Brant?"

He had no wish to talk about himself. "No. They died when I was eighteen."

Sympathy flashed in her eyes. "I'm sorry. Any brothers or sisters?"

His jaw tightened. "A brother. And before you ask, he's younger than me by a couple of years." He looked at his watch and stood up. "Come on. Let's go. It's getting late."

For a moment, surprise mixed with hurt appeared in her eyes, then cynicism took over. "Got a date, no doubt."

"No doubt." He didn't tell her he was getting together with his two best mates for dinner, though Flynn and Damien would no doubt find it amusing that they were to be his "date" this evening.

Not that he'd tell them. The three of them had grown up together on the same street in this town—had shared everything from stories of their first kiss to their first million—but Kia Benton was one thing he wasn't about to share with his rich and successful friends.

"Phillip Reid, how could you!" Kia exclaimed the next day as she swept into his study. She'd been phoning him on and off since returning from the art exhibition yesterday. He hadn't answered, but she suspected he'd been at home. He'd been feeling low so she'd given him a reprieve, but now she had a few words to say to him whether he still felt bad or not.

He looked up and winced. "What can I say, Kia? I'm sorry."

She stopped right in front of his desk. "I don't like being used," she said through gritted teeth.

His dark brows drew together. "I wasn't... I didn't mean..."

"Yes, you did." She slapped the box containing the diamond necklace down in front of him. "Don't try and fool me, Phillip. You gave me this because you knew Lynette was going to be at the party. And then you had Brant dance with me so she'd see who you'd brought as your partner. And to top things off, you tell everyone we're engaged and leave me high and dry to field all sorts of questions."

He looked thoroughly shamefaced and embarrassed. "I really *am* sorry. I didn't mean for it to go so far."

She was nowhere near ready to forgive him. Not after what she'd been through. "And yesterday? What happened to coming to the art exhibition with me?"

He swallowed hard as he leaned back in his wheelchair. "I'm sorry. I just wasn't up to going out." Then he looked confused. "Didn't Brant take you? He said he would."

"Yes, but I'd rather have gone by myself," she said sourly, preferring not to think about how much she'd enjoyed herself. She had to remember Brant could charm *any* woman into having a good time.

A speculative look came into Phillip's eyes. "Are you upset because I didn't go? Or because Brant did?"

Kia tensed, then forced herself to relax. "It's awkward spending time with one's boss," she said, avoiding a direct answer.

"You don't mind spending time with me."

She shrugged. "You're different."

"Look, if there's something between you two—"

Somehow she managed to hide her panic. "Don't be an idiot, Phillip. And, by the way, what's the deal about my security alarm? I don't remember giving either of you permission to put one in my place."

Phillip frowned, falling for the diversion. "It was the only thing to do, seeing you're my… er…fiancée. Brant would have been suspicious otherwise."

Her teeth set on edge. "Engaged or not, I am *not* some feeble female who can't take care of myself," she said with more bravado than she'd felt the other night after the robbery. "And if Brant thinks he—"

"So this *is* about Brant?" Phillip said, pushing his wheelchair back from the desk, looking very much the all-knowing male now that the heat had been taken off him.

She realized she'd given too much away. "Phillip, will you stop this. I don't know what's come over you today."

He wheeled his chair around the desk and toward her. "He gets to you, doesn't he?"

She gave a hollow laugh. "Of course not."

"And I've gone and spoiled it for you by telling everyone you're my fiancée." He stopped a few feet in front of her and thumped his hands on the armrests in helpless anger. "Hell. This is all such a bloody mess."

"That's an understatement." She just wished he'd stopped to think things through before making drastic announcements like they were engaged. "The question is, what are we going to do about it?"

He looked up at her, his expression thoroughly wretched. "I'm not sure."

"This can't go on, Phillip."

"I know. God, we were just supposed to be a couple for *one* date."

Sympathy started to soften her. "Phillip, you didn't know Lynette's father was going to be at that dinner."

"Yeah, but I knew he shared the same business circles. Dammit, I shouldn't have asked you to continue with the charade after that. It wasn't fair of me." He looked down at his leg and his lips twisted. "Pity the accident got in the way and ruined everything. But this…" He gestured at the plaster from toe to thigh. "I *know* Lynette. She would've convinced herself that I needed her. And then she would have convinced *me*. I couldn't let that happen." He took a shuddering breath. "She deserves better than a cripple for the rest of her life."

"Oh, Phillip." She crouched down in front of his wheelchair. "Don't say that. A limp does *not* make you a cripple."

He took a deep breath. "Sorry. I'm just full of self-pity today."

"Look," she said, thinking hard. "Let's wait until after Christmas, then we'll make an announcement that things didn't work out after all."

His eyes lit up, then drooped just as quick. "But your name will end up being mud. No one will care about the details, especially not the press. They'll just know you broke off the engagement during a bad time for me." He grimaced. "I'm sorry, Kia. I never meant for any of this to happen."

She squeezed his hand, trying not to think about all this being made public to the people of Darwin. "Let's ride it out, Phillip. In the meantime, we'll carry on for another week until Christmas. I heard you tell Mary that you were going home to Queensland for the holidays anyway. That'll give us some breathing space."

Intense relief surged across his face. "Good idea."

All at once Kia couldn't help but think that Brant would never let anyone else sort out his problems for him the way Phillip was doing here. Brant would have taken charge and done what he had to do. Actually, on second thought, he would never have gotten himself in this situation in the first place. Brant relied on no one except himself. He needed no one.

Just like her.

"Don't let him get to you, Kia."

She feigned ignorance. "Who?"

"Brant."

She pretended to be unconcerned. "I wish you'd stop implying that there's something going on between me and Brant. There isn't. End of story."

Is it? Phillip's eyes asked, but she promptly looked away. She wasn't about to tell him she suspected he was right.

The next week leading up to Christmas proved difficult for Kia. Not only was she extremely busy tidying things up at work so that she could enjoy their two-week closure over the holidays, but Brant seemed to sense something amiss between her and Phillip. She had the funny feeling he was homing in for the kill.

Then, just as she thought she might be able to relax, the airline phoned at the exact moment Brant walked into her office. They were checking to see if there was anything else they could do to assist Phillip on his trip to Queensland tomorrow.

Kia tried to sound as if she were talking to a client. She didn't want Brant to know she wasn't joining Phillip at this stage. "Thank you, but I believe everything's under control."

"What about on arrival in Brisbane?" the woman persisted on the other end of the line. "Can we arrange transport from the airport?"

"That's kind of you, but there will be someone to meet him," she said, then could have kicked herself when the look in Brant's eyes sharpened.

"That's fine then. But please let us know if there's anything we can do."

"Thank you, I will." Kia hung up, swallowed, then planted a polite smile on her face. "Can I help you, Mr. Matthews?"

His mouth thinned. "You can't keep calling me 'mister' for the next twenty years."

She kept a reign on her temper. "Who knows where any of us will be by then?"

"You'll be married to Phillip, of course."

She'd forgotten that was what he'd think. "Yes, of course."

"Who was on the telephone just now?"

Her heart thumped as she quickly began to tidy up some papers. "Oh, no one you should worry about."

A pair of hands flattened on the desk in front of her, stilling her. "That was someone from the airline, wasn't it?"

She drew a shaky breath and looked up into blue eyes that were riveted on her face. The caress of his warm breath on her cheeks stirred her senses. "Yes."

"So you're not on the same flight as Phillip?" he demanded, shooting each word at her with the precision of gunfire.

"No."

"Are you catching another flight?"

"Yes." To Adelaide.

"To Queensland?"

She lifted her chin in the air and decided she'd had enough of this. "I'm not going to Queensland. I'm spending Christmas with my family in Adelaide."

He leaned in that little bit closer. "So you're not spending Christmas with your new fiancé?"

She resisted shrinking back in her chair. "Not this year, no."

"Why?"

"What do you mean why?"

Anger flared in his eyes as he pushed himself back from the desk and straightened. "It's usual for an engaged couple to spend Christmas together."

"We're not a usual couple." She realized what she said too late. "I'd already made other arrangements," she pointed out as she slowly began to breathe again.

An odd glint appeared in his eyes. "I'd have thought you wouldn't want to let him out of your sight."

"I trust Phillip," she said, slightly puzzled by his question. It wasn't as though Phillip would be out nightclubbing every night. Now if it was Brant who was her fiancé…

"But do you trust Lynette Kelly?" he purred.

Shock ran through her. Had he guessed that Lynette still had feelings for Phillip? Did he know things hadn't really been settled between them?

"Lynette and Phillip are no longer an item," she

said coolly, and before he could say anything further she handed him a piece of paper. "I believe this belongs to you, Mr. Matthews."

His face hardened. "Kia, I swear if you call me Mr. Matthews one more time…" He trailed off as he opened the slip of paper. His head shot up. "What's this?"

"A check for my security alarm." She'd rung the man who'd come to her home only to find out the bill had already been paid.

Cynicism entered his eyes. "Forget it. You paid for it by coming to the art exhibition, remember?"

Yes, so why did she deserve that mocking look in his eyes? "I'm sorry, I don't see it that way. Not even as Phillip's fiancée."

"My offer was non-negotiable." He ripped it in two.

She got to her feet and walked to a cabinet too close to Brant to get her purse. "Fine. I'll write another one and give it to Phillip."

"No need for drama, Kia. Let it go."

"Mr. Matthews, if you think you can do what you like—"

He captured her arm with his warm hand, sending a slew of shivers racing over her spine. "Listen, if I did what I'd really like—"

"Is everything all right in here?"

Kia drew a ragged breath before she looked up to see Phillip had wheeled to the office door and was looking at them in concern. She stepped sideways and Brant dropped his hand.

Somehow she planted a stiff smile on her lips. "Yes, everything's fine. I was just reminding Mr. Matthews that you're going to Queensland tomorrow."

"The name's Brant," Brant snapped and stormed out of the office.

Phillip raised his brows as he looked at Kia. "Sure you don't want to come with me tomorrow? It might be safer."

Kia shook her head. There was no place on

earth safe for her. Not another state. Not another country. No, she'd just have to polish her armor and pray that Brant had better things to do on Christmas Eve than harass her.

And if she believed that, then maybe Santa Claus really did exist.

Five

Kia saw Phillip off at Darwin airport the next morning, then returned to the office to finish up some work before doing some last-minute Christmas shopping. She found Brant in Phillip's office, riffling through some papers on his desk.

He looked up when she appeared in the doorway, and his eyes darkened when he saw her. "You're back," he said as if she'd returned just for him.

And suddenly she knew she had. Despite all

the attraction she *didn't* want to feel for this man, she still felt it. Her armor was paper-thin at best.

"Yes," she murmured, willing him to come to her. To pull her into his arms. To make love to her. Long moments crept by, and she saw the struggle on his face to resist doing that very thing.

He cleared his throat. "Phil's plane get off okay?"

Phillip. Her so-called fiancé wasn't gone half an hour and she was ready to fall into bed with Brant. Dear God, why did this man have such a hold over her? She hated it. She would fight against it…with every fiber of her being.

Her gaze dropped to the paperwork in his hands. "Can I help you?" she asked, injecting cool disapproval in her tone.

His face closed up. "I was looking for the Robertson file." He went back to searching through the papers. "Phil was supposed to do some work on it."

"He did. I just have to finish typing some notes, then you can have it. Give me an hour and I'll get it to you."

"Fine." He strode around the desk and came toward her, all business now. "I'll be in my office."

She stepped back and moved to her desk before he could come anywhere near her. He sent her a mocking smile as he passed by. Well, he could mock, she told herself as she sat down and opened up the file. It wouldn't get her into his bed any faster.

Or at all.

An hour later she hurried down the hallway to his office, determined to leave the paperwork with his PA, only Evelyn was nowhere to be seen. He must have heard her in the outer office, because a few seconds later he called out to bring it in to him.

She swallowed hard, not wanting to go into his inner sanctum when no one else seemed to be around.

"Kia?"

She straightened her shoulders and walked forward. For all its luxury, she may as well have been walking into a prison cell.

"How did you know it was me?" she said.

He gave her a look that told her he always knew when she was around. "Bring it over here," he said, putting down his pen and leaning back in his chair as if she were about to put on a show and he didn't want to miss a second of it.

She hesitated. Her legs felt like jelly. Then she moved forward, and just as she'd known it would, his gaze slid over her blue tailored skirt and white silky blouse. She could see him mentally stripping the clothes from her body, piece by piece.

She was wishing that she hadn't discarded her jacket before coming in here. At least then she wouldn't have the urge to cover up the tight feeling in her nipples, and her arms wouldn't be goose-bumping in reaction.

She put the correspondence on his desk. The hint of sandalwood aftershave filled the air and stirred her senses. "I'll be leaving now. I want to finish some Christmas shopping this afternoon."

"When are you off to Adelaide?"

"Tomorrow morning."

"You'll miss Phil, no doubt?" It was a question, not a statement. Those eyes watched her like a cat stalking a mouse, waiting for her to make one wrong move. Well, she didn't much like cheese.

She pasted on a smile. "Naturally, but I'll be kept pretty busy. My mother loves to put on a bash at Christmas," she chatted on nervously, until all at once she saw a hint of bleakness in his eyes that clutched at her heart. She spoke before she could stop herself. "What about you, Brant? Any plans for Christmas?"

"So you remembered my name, eh?" Then he straightened in his chair. "A friend has invited me around for Christmas dinner, but I'm not sure I'll go yet. I've got too much work."

"What about your brother?" she said, curious to see his reaction again.

"What about him?" he snapped, his eyes turning colder than winter.

She swallowed. "I just thought—"

"Look, I don't want anything to do with my brother and that's the way I like it."

She took a step back. "Oh."

Tension filled the air and hung there for a few seconds before Brant appeared to make himself relax. Then he leaned over and took something out of the drawer in his desk. "I have a Christmas present for you."

Her heart jumped in her throat. "A…a present?"

He held out the small package toward her. "I gave Evelyn one, too. Can't let the best two PAs in town not know they're appreciated."

His tone held something biting, though she

knew it was intended for *her,* not Evelyn. But she accepted the gift anyway. Phillip had given Evelyn a present, so what was wrong in Brant giving *her* one?

Then she met his eyes and she knew that everything *was* wrong about this. This wasn't because of her work. It was because he wanted her. This was a man wanting his woman and telling her in the only way he could.

Her hands shook as she undid the wrapping paper and lifted the lid on the small box inscribed with the top jeweler's name in Australia. She gasped when she saw the small medallion nestled on a velvet bed amongst the gold chain.

"It's not a diamond necklace," he said with cutting emphasis, "but it should keep you safe on your journey home."

"It's a St. Christopher medallion," she murmured, pushing his cynicism aside, touched by the charming gift. "Thank you. It's lovely. I'll make sure I put it on before I leave."

"Let me," he rasped.

Her breath hitched. Could she bear to have him touch her, no matter how briefly? Oh, how she wanted this. Was this one little thing too much to ask?

"Thank you," she whispered, her voice shaky.

He came around the desk and took the present out of her hands. "Turn around."

She did, and for a long moment everything in the room went quiet. Her heart skipped a beat. She could feel him standing there looking at her, his warm breath flowing over the nape of her neck, making her light-headed. If she leaned back, his arms would snake around her and then… *Oh, for heaven's sake, Kia, get a grip on yourself,* she scolded inwardly.

The package rustled and then the gold chain came around her neck. The medallion lovingly touched the base of her throat, cooling her skin.

He placed his hands on her shoulders and slowly turned her around to face him.

"Merry Christmas, Kia," he said hoarsely, moving in to kiss her.

She lifted her lips. She had to. An avalanche could be coming their way and she'd still wait for that kiss.

His lips touched hers briefly. So brief that it should have been a chaste kiss. But every pore of her skin felt him there, acknowledged him, cried out for more.

He moved back and their eyes locked. Her throat seemed to close at the intense desire written in his eyes and the struggle within him not to take her.

He stepped back with a low sound in his throat that seemed to wrench from deep inside him. It broke the spell of the moment.

She drew in a shaky breath. "Merry Christmas to you, too, Brant."

A muscle knotted in his jaw as he walked back around to the other side of the desk. "I hope you get everything you want."

If ever there was a time for *not* getting what she wished for, it was now. When she wanted *him*.

She spun around and hurried toward the door, needing to get out of there.

"Have a good holiday, Kia...even without your fiancé."

Kia stopped to glance at him and saw the look in his eyes was harder than ever. She tensed. They were right back where they'd started. And that was fine with her.

"I intend to," she said coolly and left the room.

Kia normally loved being with her family at Christmas. Neighbors dropped by for a Christmas drink in the morning, and her sister, Melanie, came around for lunch with her husband and young son. The weather usually proved to be hot at this time of year, so a variety of seafood and salads was the order of the day, followed by an English-style trifle that her mother made to perfection. A treat her stepfather loved. All very normal and comforting. Usually.

So why did she feel as though something was missing this year? It was a nagging thought inside her that remained there throughout the day and began again when she woke on Boxing Day. She felt restless. As if she should be some place else but didn't know where.

It wasn't until a barbecue lunch in the backyard, where she was playing peekaboo with her six-month-old nephew, that she looked up and her heart dropped to her feet. The laughter died on her lips. And suddenly she knew what had been missing. *Brant.* He stood near the corner of the house, watching her, his eyes piercing the distance between them. Her family faded from her mind.

"Who's that?" she heard her mother say, and all at once Kia realized he *was* there. He wasn't a figment of her imagination. And here she was dressed in denim jeans and a stretch knit top, far from the businesslike persona she kept for the office and even for Phillip.

She handed Dominic to her sister and jumped up. "It's okay, Mum. It's one of my bosses. I'll be right back."

She raced toward him, her hand going to her throat as something occurred to her. Something must be wrong. Terribly wrong.

"Phillip?" she croaked as she got closer.

Irritation flickered across his face, then disappeared. "Relax. He's okay, as far as I know."

She moistened her lips. "Then what are you doing here?" It had to be something important if he'd flown from the north of the continent to the south, over three thousand kilometers.

"The Anderson project needs redoing. Phillip must have been having a bad day when he met with them, because he got all their instructions wrong. If we don't present them with another option by Thursday morning, we lose the account."

Kia remembered she'd been a bit uneasy about that particular project. She'd even said something to Phillip about it and gotten her head snapped off at the time.

"I've got a ton of work ahead of me and I need a PA."

She frowned. "What about Evelyn?"

He smiled without humor. "Remember that medallion I gave her that was supposed to keep her safe? It didn't work. She came down with a stomach virus yesterday morning. It looks like she'll be out of action for the rest of the week."

She grimaced. "Poor Evelyn." But why did she suspect he was pleased about this? Not about Evelyn being sick but about needing *her* as replacement. Probably because he was enjoying ruining her holiday like this.

Her eyebrow lifted. "Why not hire a temp?"

"This project is too important, Kia. The

company will still survive if we lose them as a client, but I'm not sure about Phil. How do you think he's going to feel if he finds out what's happened? He's pretty down at the moment." He had her with that and they both knew it. "No, I need you to come back to Darwin and help me out. I flew down last night and I've got a jet waiting at the airport now. I'll pay you triple time, of course."

She waved a dismissive hand. "I don't care about the money."

"Then think of it as repayment for the security alarm."

Her shoulders tensed. "You said that was already paid in full," she reminded him, though she still had every intention of paying off the debt herself, and in cash. "Or is this one of those debts that only seem to compound interest?"

A half smile crossed his face. "Perhaps."

"Kia, love," her mother's voice said behind

her, and Kia froze. "Why not bring your boss over to meet the family?"

Kia leaned toward Brant. "Please don't mention Phillip," she whispered.

"What?" he muttered.

"They don't know about him." She saw his flash of surprise just before she swung around to face her mother to make the introductions.

But surprised or not, he soon recovered. Kia watched him turning on the charm, but she knew he'd be asking some hard questions when they were alone.

"I can certainly see where Kia gets her looks," he told her mother with a warm smile that only seemed to be available for other women.

Kia mentally rolled her eyes, but she had to admit her father would never have married her mother if she hadn't been a looker. Her mother had the warmest of natures, too. She hadn't deserved to be treated so badly.

Marlene blushed with pleasure. "Thank you, Mr. Matthews."

He darted a wry glance at Kia that said *like mother, like daughter* for calling him "mister," then turned back to her mother. "Call me Brant."

Marlene nodded. "Well, Brant. Come over and meet the rest of Kia's family." She slipped her arm through his and began walking toward the others. "Have you had lunch yet?"

"Yes, but thanks for the offer."

"Then have a drink. It's Christmas, after all." She gave a warm smile. "Besides, we want to get to know Kia's boss." She leaned slightly closer to Brant. "We worry about her up there in Darwin by herself."

He smiled. "No need to worry. We're keeping a very close eye on her," he said, and Kia's heart lurched at the hidden meaning behind those words. Suddenly her jeans felt too tight and her pink top too skimpy.

"Oh, I'm so pleased to hear that." They reached the others. "Brant, this is my husband,

Gerald." The two men sized each other up and shook hands. "And this is Kia's sister, Melanie. And her husband…"

Kia gritted her teeth as she watched the females succumb to Brant's charm like a line of dominoes toppling over. The men weren't so accommodating at first, but before long Brant had them eating out of the palm of his hand, too. Did this man know no bounds?

"So why have you come to see Kia?" her stepfather asked, and Kia saw that maybe Brant hadn't quite charmed the older man as much as she'd thought. She smiled at Gerald, loving him all the more for his protection.

"There's a major problem at the office and I need Kia's help. She's been working on the project with Ph—" He hesitated, then smiled at Kia. "She knows it by heart and I can't do it without her. I have no choice but to beg her to return to the office with me. Believe me, I wouldn't ask her if it wasn't important."

"Of course you wouldn't," her mother said. She glanced at her daughter. "Darling, are you still doing your studies?"

Brant's ears pricked up. "Studies?"

Kia groaned inwardly. "I'm learning Chinese."

"And she's doing very well, too," Marlene said proudly. "She's got quite a knack for languages and is already fluent in French and Italian."

Brant regarded her with a speculative gaze. "You really are a mystery at times, aren't you?" he said, but she could see a slight hardness back in those eyes.

He glanced at his watch. "We'd better be going."

She nodded. "I'll just get my things together." She left him talking to the others, a little regretful that she hadn't had more time to spend with her family. But, on the other hand, helping out in a time of crisis was a small sacrifice to make for the good of the company.

Then she thought of working alone with Brant when they got back to Darwin and she pushed aside a level of excitement that had nothing to do with the challenge of the project and everything to do with the man himself. She swallowed hard. Correction. This wasn't a small sacrifice. This was going to be a *big* one.

Her hands shook as she quickly showered before slipping into a floral-print shirtdress with a short-sleeved jacket that was easy-wearing for travel but stylish enough for the office. Not bothering with stockings, she stepped into high-heeled sandals that complimented her long, tanned legs. A light touch of makeup and a quick deft of her hand to twist her hair up and she was ready. For battle. For Brant.

"Perhaps you can explain something to me," he said once they were seated in the plush jet and were heading back to Darwin.

Warning shivers started going up and down her spine. "Like what?"

"Like why you didn't tell your family about Phillip?"

She tried not to flinch. "Oh. That."

"Yes. *That.*"

Her cheeks reddened. "I just want to be sure, that's all."

He straightened in his seat, on full alert now. "You're not sure?"

"Yes, of course I am," she said quickly. "It's just that it all happened so fast. I don't want my family to worry and I know they would."

A moment's pause, then he said, "Tell me. Do you love Phil?"

If she hesitated, she was lost. "Yes."

His jaw clenched. "When do you plan on telling them?"

"When the time is right. Thank you for not saying anything today. It would have been… awkward."

God, she didn't like lying, but what else could she do? If she told the truth, Brant would go all out to seduce her. She'd be putty in his hands and she had no doubt she'd enjoy it. But that would be just a physical release. It wouldn't be enough. She needed more from a man than a quick roll in the hay.

Besides, this wasn't just about her. She couldn't give the game away yet. How could she tell Brant the truth and dump all this on Phillip's shoulders without giving him any warning? She didn't think she was better than Phillip, but she couldn't do to him what he'd done to her. No, she'd have to wait until he returned to the office in another two weeks. She just hoped she survived until then.

"I'm sure they'd be happy for you," Brant said. "Phillip's a great catch."

"Yes." She ignored the cynical tone to his voice, not quite up to verbally fencing with him right now.

About to look away, something about him grabbed her attention and she was surprised to catch a bleak look in his eyes before his gaze dropped to the papers in his lap. An odd feeling of sympathy caught at her heartstrings. Was his coming to fetch her more than just the problem at work? Had he been feeling lonely, despite a "friend" inviting him for Christmas lunch?

"Did you have a nice Christmas, Brant?"

His gaze shot toward her. "Why?"

"I just wondered."

His smooth look made her wish she'd kept her mouth shut. "Yes, I was kept very…busy."

She winced inwardly. "I see." He was a womanizer, so he'd been with a woman most likely. She understood him only too well. He was just like her father.

Nine o'clock that evening Brant decided to wrap things up for the day. Exhausted, he eased back in his leather chair and flexed his fingers. He could hear the clack of the keyboard in the outer office and knew that no matter how tired he was he would still want Kia Benton.

Even today, when he'd caught her offguard at her mother's place, she'd made his stomach knot with desire. Hell, he could still remember how he'd felt when he'd seen her dressed so casually in those tight jeans that lovingly hugged her body. She'd looked so different. So carefree and friendly.

And when he saw her with that toddler in her arms…it was as if he'd been seeing a glimpse of the future.

His and Kia's future.

For the first time since Julia, he imagined actually being with a woman. Having more than just a physical connection. But not even Julia had roused the same level of yearning that had ripped through him today when he'd seen Kia.

But Kia was only out for one thing.

The woman needed money the way she needed air to breathe. Her assertion that she loved Phillip had sounded hollow to his ears, but even if he were tempted to forget it, he only had to remember that while her beautiful mouth might lie, the camera hadn't. The self-satisfied smirk she'd been wearing in that photograph of her and Phillip had said it all: Kia Benton had caught her man.

He straightened in his chair, disgust tightening his mouth. So how could he even think about Kia on a deeper level? It was all this damn Christmas stuff, that's what it was. It stirred too many memories of when he was growing up.

Not that he could complain about his childhood. His parents had been the best, practically adopting the other kids in the street. Many a time Flynn had taken refuge in Brant's house when his father had been too drunk to care. And Damien's parents hadn't meant to be so distant from their son, leaving the small boy starving for parental affection. Brant knew if it hadn't been for Barbara and Jack Matthews, his two friends may not have turned out as well as they had. It had bonded the three of them together.

Like brothers.

His mouth tightened. Unlike his own flesh and blood, who had stolen his fiancée.

He got to his feet and walked to the doorway, pushing aside the thought of his younger brother, Royce, as he forced his mind back to the business at hand.

For a minute he stood watching Kia's fingers fly over the keyboard while she continued to type up the reams of paperwork needed to get the project back on track. He didn't know what Phil had been thinking, putting together a package like that. It had been totally wrong, full of errors and not feasible.

"You knew, didn't you?" he said, coming into the room. "That the presentation was all wrong?"

She blinked in surprise, then nodded. "I had

an idea. I mentioned it to Phillip, but he thought he was right, so I left it at that." She shrugged. "He's the boss."

"And so am I. You should have come to me."

She arched a brow. "And tell you what exactly? That my boss wasn't thinking straight because he'd lost the use of his leg and now I was telling him he was beginning to lose his mind, too?"

"I admire your loyalty, Kia, but next time save us both some stress and just tell me about it. I won't go running to Phil, but I'll find a way around it. If Phil's not coping, we need to get him some help."

She sighed. "Yes, you're right."

He went to speak, to tell her how Phillip's judgment was sometimes suspect and had caused problems before, but then he remembered whose fiancée she was.

"Right. Let's call it a night. Would you like to get a bite to eat on the way home?"

Suddenly he didn't want to go home alone. He had nothing waiting for him there. And no doubt they'd still have all those sappy Christmas movies on television.

She began stacking papers. "No, thanks. The pizza was more than enough."

"We ate that hours ago."

She looked up with a rueful gleam in her eyes. "I'm still full from Christmas lunch yesterday."

That gleam hit him right in his chest. There was a warmth in her eyes whenever she spoke of her family that just didn't correspond with the cold, callous player he knew her to be.

He stared at her for a minute more, then spun around and went back into his office. He supposed even criminals had their good points.

Six

The next day Kia would have loved to concentrate on the job at hand, but with everyone still on vacation, just being alone with Brant in the executive suite left her scarcely daring to breathe. It was the reason she'd insisted on working from her own office at the other end of the floor. Away from him. Away from temptation. And out of the sexual firing line.

He'd seen right through her, but she'd still held her head high when she told him she felt more comfortable at her own desk. It had been the truth, after all.

"Bring me the next twenty pages when you've finished them," was all he'd said mid-afternoon, the glint in his eyes telling her that even a crucial project couldn't surpass this attraction between them.

"Aye, aye, sir," she'd snapped, spinning on her heels and leaving the room, but not before she'd seen the arrogance in his eyes. Okay, so he was the boss, but that didn't mean he had to "boss" her about. It only made her madder, and ever since, her fingers had been flying across the keyboard, wanting to finish the twenty pages as soon as possible so she could march into his office and slam them down on the desk.

And that's exactly what she did—in half the time it normally took. But to her amazement, when she got to his office, he was nowhere to be seen. The adrenaline that had given her fingers strength dissipated, leaving her drained and ludicrously disappointed. She sighed. The considerate thing for him to do would have been to tell her he was going out.

She placed the papers in the center of his desk and turned to go back to her office. A figure in the doorway made her jump. For a minute she thought it was Brant. Adjusting her eyes she realized it was Lynette Kelly.

Kia breathed in deeply, her heart not quite settling back into place. "Lynette, what are you doing here?"

Lynette blushed as she took a few steps into the office. "Oh, hello, Kia."

She looked so nervous Kia felt sorry for her. "Can I help you?" she asked gently.

"Er…I need to see Phillip. I called him at home, but there was no answer. I thought he might be here."

"I'm sorry. He's not." Lynette's face fell and Kia spoke before thinking. "He's gone home to Queensland for a couple of weeks."

The other woman's eyes widened. "Without you?"

Kia's gaze darted away then back. "I had to stay here. To work."

"Oh." Her shoulders slumped. She turned away. "I guess I'd better—" She spun back. "Kia, do you really love Phillip? I mean, like a woman should love a man? Please, I need to know."

There was such anguish in her eyes, guilt stabbed Kia in the heart.

"Kia, he needs me. I know he does. I love him with all my heart and I'm swallowing my pride in front of you and begging you to tell me the truth."

Kia couldn't stand Lynette's pain any longer. It just wasn't right to keep the other woman in the dark. She owed it to her—and to Phillip— to help straighten things out.

"No, Lynette. I don't love Phillip. Not in that way."

"Thank God." Lynette swayed, then quickly

gathered herself, blinking back tears. When she'd recovered, a crease formed between her eyes and she looked confused. "So why did you get engaged?"

Kia told her the truth and explained how one thing had led to another. "I'm sorry for all the pain we've put you through, Lynette. I was just trying to help Phillip."

"Do you…?" Lynette swallowed. "Do you think he still loves me?"

"I know he does."

Hope filled Lynette's eyes and made them shine. "I have to go to him."

Kia nodded. Behind the other woman's delicate appearance, she sensed a strength of character she suspected would surprise Phillip. "If he gives you a hard time, tell him I said he's a fool."

Lynette quickly hugged her. "I hope you find someone for you soon."

"I'm not sure I want anyone," Kia said with

a small smile. The only person who had ever really affected her was Brant. And he…well, there was nothing more to say there.

Lynette left the room, so happy she looked as if she were walking on air. Kia smiled as relief swept through her that she'd told the other woman of Phillip's love. It was in Lynette's hands now.

Just then, the hairs on the back of Kia's neck stood to attention. Even before she turned toward the connecting door she was certain Brant would be standing there.

And he was. He'd been in the small conference room the whole time. A fear such as she'd never known skittered under her skin. Primal fear. Sexual fear. She only had to look at the anger in his eyes to know he had overheard.

"Um…Brant. I didn't know you were there."

For a moment the air hung between them like a sheet of humidity.

"So the gold digger's conscience got the

better of her, did it?" he sneered, leaning against the doorjamb, about as laid-back as a crocodile lazing in the sun.

She sucked in a sharp breath. "Gold digger?" *Was he crazy?* "Are you talking about *me?*"

"Too bad, sweetheart. You missed out on marriage this time, but I'm sure you can find another man to fall for that innocent act."

"Wh-what?" She had no idea what he was talking about.

"Don't deny it. I saw your picture in a magazine. Even the journalist could tell a fortune hunter when he saw one. In fact, he remarked on how you'd hooked one of the Australia's richest bachelors."

Was she really hearing this? "That *journalist*—and I use the word loosely—has got it in for me because I refused to go out with him. He's just trying to make me look bad." She'd felt ill when she'd seen the photograph and the comment he'd made.

"Really?" Brant's eyes said he didn't believe her. "Even if that's the case, I heard you on the telephone. My ears don't deceive me."

She frowned. "Telephone?"

"That's right. When I came back from Paris I heard you bragging to someone on the phone about it being as easy to fall in love with a rich man than a poor one." His top lip curled. "The next thing, you were Phillip's shadow and engaged to him."

She tried to think. Then it hit her. "I was talking to Gerald…my stepfather. It's a joke between us. Good Lord. So this is why you've been a pig to me since I first met you? You thought I was marrying Phillip for his *money?*"

He made a harsh sound. "You were quick to take the diamond necklace from him."

"He asked me to wear it to the Christmas party. I gave it back the next day. Ask him if you don't believe me."

Something flickered in his eyes. "The Porsche?"

"My father gave it to me. He deals in cars, remember?" Her heart twinged. "He likes his 'Barbie' to come with accessories."

For a moment there was a flash of sympathy, then his face hardened. "If you dislike your father so much, why take the car?"

"He offered and I thought why not? I figure the man owes me for all he's put me through. If he wants to give me a Porsche, I'm taking the Porsche. There's nothing wrong with that." She paused. "Anyway, if I wanted money, I only have to ask him for some…not that I would. He's got enough money to keep me in luxury for the rest of my life. Unfortunately it comes with a price."

A tic beat in his jaw. "Even if all that's true, you're obviously very good at conning people. You've been living a lie."

She winced. "For Phillip's sake."

"And for your own. You used him just as much as he used you."

Her chin lifted. He was so conceited. "Now why would I do that?" she said, then realized it was a challenge.

Suddenly he turned and closed the connecting door behind him. "To keep *us* apart."

Her eyes darted to the doorknob where his hand still rested. "Us? There's nothing between us."

He strode across the room to the main office door. "Lying again, Kia?" He shut that door too. Then he turned back toward her in the middle of the room.

Her knees began to shake. "Er...what are you doing?"

"What do you think I'm doing?" His voice flowed over her like liquid silk.

Her throat went dry. "You're playing games with me."

"No game, Kia. Far from it."

She straightened her shoulders. "Brant, stop it. This is ridiculous. You're my boss. I'm—"

"About to be kissed," he murmured, stopping right in front of her. He didn't touch her. Didn't reach out. He just stood there, looking at her. And what she saw melted every bone in her body. He was still angry, but oh, God, he wanted her.

She licked her lips. "Brant, I—"

"I'm so angry with you right now I'm either going to swear or kiss you."

She tried to step back.

He grabbed her arm to prevent her from moving, his touch shooting desire to every region of her body. "And then I'm going to take the clothes off that delicious body of yours and taste all of you."

She felt the room twirl around her. "I don't know if this is a good idea."

He pulled her closer, his pupils darkening. "I've waited too long already."

A ripple of anticipation ran through her as she watched his head lower…watched those lips come closer…and when he touched her, she could no longer deny him or herself. Every moment from the minute she'd met him had been rushing headlong toward this kiss. Ever since her first look at him in this very office, nothing else had mattered, nothing but wanting to feel the consuming pressure of his lips on hers, as they were doing now.

At last.

The kiss still took her by surprise. She expected him to plunder and ravish her on the carpet, but he didn't, and she soon forgot all about his anger as the velvet warmth of his mouth stirred every nerve ending on her lips, before he used his tongue to slide inside her.

And there he stayed, exploring the soft, sensitized recesses of her mouth until she thought she might fuse with him. But she wanted him closer. She wrapped her arms around his neck and cupped the back of his head to hold him to her. It felt so good to be like this with him. This was where she belonged. If only for a short while.

Raising his mouth from hers, he gazed deeply into her eyes, so deep that she suddenly worried he might see the real her. Not the outside person but the inside person. The person who didn't know how she was going to handle this man.

"What's the matter?" he said, watching her.

"Um…nothing." Her gaze darted down to his chest, lowering her eyelids, briefly covering her face from him. She wanted to remain like this and not let him see her thoughts. She needed to keep something of herself to herself.

And then he took her arms from around his neck and put them at her sides. He lifted her chin, holding her gaze. "I won't let you hold back from me," he warned softly.

She took a shaky breath. "You won't *let* me?"

"No." He reached out and undid the top button of her dress, and suddenly she didn't have the strength to argue with him. She stood there and let him undress her. She *wanted* him to do it. *Wanted* him to undo all the buttons and feel his touch on her skin. *Wanted* to give all of herself to him.

His hands were sure and never missed a beat as they slid down from one button to the next, opening the material wider, more fully. For him.

She could see the pulse in his neck thumping wildly and she wanted to reach out and run her finger over it. Touching him would be like throwing a match onto kerosene.

He pushed the material off her shoulders and let it slide down her arms, down her body, to the carpet. She heard him groan as she stood there in a lacy bra, bikini panties, no stockings, and high-heeled sandals. For a moment she wished she'd worn them. It may have put up a barrier.

But who was she kidding? Nothing was going to stop this. She didn't want it to stop, God help her.

"I like the color peach on you," he murmured, his eyes flaring with hot desire. "It flatters you."

She moaned and whispered, "Touch me," and he suddenly swung her in his arms, carrying her over to the large mahogany desk. With one hand he swept the papers aside, then planted her in the middle of it. Her stomach somersaulted as he stood looking down at her.

"I've fantasized you like this for weeks," he murmured, reaching out to twine his fingers in her hair, loosening the blonde strands at the nape of her neck. "And this," he said, lifting her hair up in his hands, then leaning forward and burying his face in her locks, inhaling deeply.

She stilled, breathing in the mingled scent of his body heat and aftershave as it soaked into her pores...until the soft peck of his lips moved to her ear, to her jawline and finally her mouth again.

Eventually he broke off the kiss. "Here, let me," he murmured, his fingers sliding under her bra straps and slowly pushing them off her shoulders.

She trembled when his palms caressed the bare skin there before slipping around to her back to undo the catch. Her bra fell away, and suddenly she was naked from the waist up. She wanted to hide, not from him but from herself. She didn't know if she could let herself go like this.

"Beautiful," he said in a gravelly voice, teasing her breasts with his hands until her breathing quickened even more and she had to close her eyes from sheer pleasure.

His head lowered, his mouth closing over one nipple, and she gasped, her breasts surging at the intimacy of it all.

"Brant!"

He pulled back, his eyes searing a path over her. And then he moved and his lips followed that same path, kissing down the center of her, teasing her belly button with the tip of his tongue before stopping at the top of her thighs.

He inhaled deeply through the thin lace, and she almost dissolved. She'd never done anything like this before. Never *let* a man do this to her. She'd had one lover in high school and nothing since.

He pushed the material to one side. "I have to taste you," he said, his fingers seeking her, opening her to him. He placed his mouth against her, and she cried out his name as his tongue darted out to taste her, explore her, tracing the shape of her, teasing the small part of her that suddenly felt as if she were about to explode.

"Oh, Brant," she moaned again. She closed her eyes as something powerful inched up inside her with every touch of his tongue. It felt so good…so right…so exquisite.

"Ooh!" She exploded with one more stroke, going up in flames like a bushfire sweeping through her, burning everything in sight, leaving nothing of her unmarked. She would never be the same again, never forget what it was like to have this man touch her like this.

And when she opened her eyes, Brant was leaning back in the chair, watching her with such possessive satisfaction that her breath caught in her throat.

Her heart gave a triple beat. She wanted to look away, only she couldn't. There'd been too much between them all these weeks. Too much longing. Too much wanting each other. They'd earned this moment between them.

Brant spoke first. "Here, let's get you dressed," he said brusquely and gently closed her legs.

"Oh, but…" She could feel her cheeks growing red as he passed her bra. "I mean… um…aren't we going to…?"

"Make love? Not yet." He stood up and helped her off the desk as intense disappointment swept through her. She went to turn away, but he held her still. "My place. Seven o'clock."

She blinked. "To-tonight?"

"Yes." He ran a finger across her lips, his eyes a mixture of need and still-deep anger. "No more waiting. For either of us. And I can't do everything I want to do to you in the office."

She swallowed, suddenly panicked by the magnitude of it all. He overwhelmed her. He made her feel things she didn't want to feel. Made her do things she *wanted* to do.

"No, I can't. I—"

"I've put my stamp on you now, Kia. You can't deny that."

She sucked in a shaky breath, very much aware he was right. "Brant, this was just a… brief interlude."

"It was a prelude," he insisted, putting his hand under her chin. "You were ready for me a minute ago," he reminded her, and she almost dissolved again.

"Yes, well…" She cleared her throat. "That was then. This is now."

His eyes darkened dangerously. "Kia, we should have been lovers weeks ago."

Her shoulders tensed. She could see his anger over Phillip still simmering beneath the surface. "Even if you hadn't thought I was with Phillip, it doesn't mean—"

"Yes, it does," he cut across her. "Have no doubts, Kia. We *would* have been lovers. You're only fooling yourself if you think otherwise."

To prove it, his hands slid around her waist and brought her close. Her body immediately arched against him, her near-naked curves tucking in against his hard contours. Heat rippled under her skin and jolted her mind into the realization that once again he was right. She pushed herself away, and thankfully he let her go, but the smoldering look in his eyes said it all.

Trying to maintain her composure, she hurried around the desk to get the rest of her clothes, feeling exposed in more ways than one. His gaze remained on her, watching her every move, and she silently shuddered as she dressed as fast as she could.

"Kia."

She did up the last button, then looked up at him. The hunger in his eyes sent a tremor through her.

"You owe this to yourself," he growled, challenge in his voice.

Kia made her way back to her office on shaky legs and collapsed onto her chair. She couldn't believe what had just happened. Had she really let herself be taken in such a way? No man had made love to her with his mouth before, though she knew it was an aspect of lovemaking that most couples enjoyed. Dear God, now she could see why.

What she hadn't expected was to come apart in Brant's hands quite the way she had. Where was her control? Her self-respect? She'd known she was a challenge to him. That he only wanted her body. So what had she done? She'd handed herself to him on a platter, that's what.

Or a desk, she corrected, feeling a blush rising up from the tips of her toes. How could she hold her head high now? Suddenly she knew she had to get out of there. She'd earned the right to leave early…in more ways than one.

Jumping to her feet, she grabbed her handbag and headed for the door. If she remained here alone with Brant, he might be tempted to take up where they'd left off and not wait for tonight.

Tonight.

You owe this to yourself, he'd said.

He was right, yet how could she turn up at his place when he thought she was a gold digger? Had thought it from the start. A woman who was mercenary enough to use men for her own advantage. That hurt.

So why did her heart turn over at the thought of *not* making love with Brant?

Brant tossed the pencil on the desk. He needed to get these reports out, but his mind kept dropping back to Kia. Could he accept she wasn't a gold digger? Her answers had made sense, but isn't that what con artists did? They conned you into believing what they wanted you to believe.

And all these weeks she'd been living a lie by pretending to be involved with Phillip. Had even let herself become engaged to him. Just as Julia had lived a lie. Until she'd run off with his own brother.

Hell. He thought he'd been hearing things when Kia had told Lynette she didn't love Phil the way a woman should love a man. She'd lied to *him,* dammit. He'd asked her straight out if she loved her fiancé and she'd said yes.

Why? Because she knew he'd have her in bed in no time, that's why. She wouldn't be able to help herself. She'd wanted to make love with him, too.

Yet how different she'd been to the experienced women he usually bedded. Women who proudly strutted their stuff. Women who took the initiative, the way he liked. Women who hadn't shattered in his arms as Kia had. Her passion, her innocence in this way, convinced him she hadn't been with a man or come alive under a man's mouth in years. That was something in her favor. Surely a gold digger wouldn't hesitate to use her body to get men to fall in love with her? Oh, hell. He just didn't know what to think anymore.

What he *did* know was that she'd been perfect. Had tasted better than perfect. It's the reason he'd held himself in check and not taken her fully as he'd ached to do. He wanted to love her slowly, take his time, make up for all those weeks of aching. Tonight he'd brand her with his body and make her his.

When he opened the door to his penthouse that evening, Brant almost forgot to breathe. The soft blue material of Kia's dress bared her tanned shoulders and arms and fell lovingly over the length of her body to just above her knees, in a simple design that would have looked plain on another woman. Yet on her it looked stunning. She couldn't look unattractive if her life depended on it.

He stepped back to allow her to enter. "Relax. I'm not going to ravish you on the spot," he said, even if the thought was more than tempting.

She moved past him in a cloud of perfume that was endlessly alluring, then stopped in the middle of the room and faced him, the light of battle entering her eyes. "That's a relief," she quipped, a becoming flush staining her cheeks.

He closed the door, knowing he could always count on her to be defiant even in the most difficult of circumstances. And this had to be the most difficult for her ever. But her uncertainty didn't change a thing. They would make love tonight.

"Take a seat while I pour you a drink." He gestured to the black leather sofa. "Gin and tonic, right?"

"Extra large."

"Oh, no, you don't," he drawled. "I don't want you to forget a moment of tonight. *I* certainly don't intend to."

She moistened her lips. "Brant, I think this is a mistake. I shouldn't have come."

"It isn't a mistake. It's called being grown-up. It's about being adults over a situation that we both clearly need to address."

Her chin rose in the air. "I thought it was

more childlike when you give in and take what you want."

"Ah, so you admit you want me," he said as he poured the drinks at the bar.

She glared at him. "I think we should leave things as they are. My being here will only complicate matters."

He picked up the glasses of liquid and walked toward her. "A complication I'll willingly embrace, if you'll pardon the pun."

She ignored that as she accepted her glass. "How do you know I won't be faking it? After all, I faked the engagement and you never knew the difference, for all your extensive experience."

"I suspected something was amiss."

Her mouth set in a stubborn line. "I did it for a reason. To help Phillip."

"And to keep me at arm's length."

"It worked."

"And now it doesn't. Accept it."

Her blue eyes lit with anger. "Look, you said

yourself that I'm a gold digger. If you want a woman tonight, why pick on me? Wouldn't any *body* do?"

His amusement deserted him. "No," he said tersely. No other woman in the world would do. It was the reason he hadn't returned any of his women friend's calls. Why he hadn't made love in weeks now. The reason he'd thrown himself into his work even harder. And why he'd been so bloody snappy with everyone lately. It just hadn't been humane that the one woman who turned him on had been involved with his business partner.

He expelled a breath he hadn't realized he'd been holding. Yes, she *had* been involved with Phil. *Had* been untouchable. *Had* been out of reach.

But she was no longer.

He nodded at the sliding glass doors. "Let's go out on the balcony. We can have dinner out there."

Her shoulders stiffened. "I'm not hungry."

"Then perhaps we should give dinner a miss?"

She immediately stepped forward and strode past him to the balcony, her set mouth telling him what she thought of that idea.

"I figured that would change your mind," he murmured, following her over to the railing, where she stood looking out over the spectacular sunset view of Mindil Beach and Darwin Harbor. It was glorious out here at any time of year, but during the beginning of the wet season, like now, he loved watching the incredible lightning displays that lit up the sky most nights.

Yet tonight the only thing he wanted to light up was the woman standing next to him. He turned to look at her. The evening sun reflected on the delicate contours of her face, giving her a special glow, making her look more beautiful.

"Do you have to look at me like that?" she said in a throaty voice, a blush creeping into her cheeks.

"Yes," he said huskily. Right now he didn't think he'd ever get enough of looking at her.

She swallowed hard. "You're not making this any easier for me."

"Nothing worthwhile is ever easy."

She turned to face him, her expression growing resentful. "That's the attraction, isn't it, Brant? You couldn't have me, so you decided you wanted me."

"I admit I like a challenge." His eyes dipped to her parted lips. "But wanting you wasn't a decision I chose to make. I took one look at you and knew the decision had already been made for me."

"How nice," she said with false sweetness.

He smiled. She could fight herself all she liked, but it wouldn't make one speck of difference. She would be in his arms tonight. And in his bed. He was sure of that.

"Shall we eat?" he said and took great pleasure in placing his hand under her elbow to lead her over to the small dining table in the middle of the balcony. Her shiver was from desire, he saw it in her eyes, and it sent a hunger for more than food racing through him. But he could wait. He wanted to savor her first.

They dined on prawn cocktail as an entrée, followed by a grilled lamb with zucchini and tomatoes that his housekeeper had made. Brant watched in amusement over Kia's attempt to go slow as she chewed each mouthful as though it was the last food she'd ever eat.

"This is very good," she said, taking another tiny bite of the lamb. "Did you cook this yourself?"

He shot her a mocking smile. "Do I look like a cook?"

She stiffened. "I don't think there's anything wrong with cooking. Lots of men like to do it."

"And lots of men like to make love," he said, purposefully seductive. "How many men have made love to you, Kia?"

She almost choked, then recovered quickly. "How many have *you* made love to?"

"I don't find men attractive. Now women, that's more my style."

Her eyes filled with derision. "I guess it's more an art form than a technique with you then."

He leaned back in his chair, curious at her remark.

She pressed on. "I'd say you've had plenty of practice having sex."

"True. But I've always practiced safe sex, so you have no worries on that score."

"I'm relieved," she said drily.

"It's important, Kia."

She sighed. "I know."

"So, Kia." He paused and took a sip of wine. "How many lovers have you had?"

"One."

He arched a brow as the muscles at the back of his neck tensed. Could she really be as innocent as all that?

She shot him a defiant look. "Hey, you asked, so don't blame me if you don't like the answer."

His eyes narrowed. "I know your game. You think I'll back off if you tell me you're inexperienced."

She placed her fork on the table. "Actually, I don't care what you think. It's the truth."

His gut clenched. "Tell me about it."

"Why should I?"

"Because I want no more secrets between us, Kia. Not in bed, anyway."

She considered him for a long moment. Then she said, "I lost my virginity at a party when I was fifteen. It was the one and only time I got drunk and I gave it away to the first boy that looked at me because my father had just gotten married and didn't want his 'plain-looking' daughter at his wedding and I needed to feel loved. He didn't even ask me my name."

She said it so matter-of-factly that he believed her. He swore under his breath.

She shrugged. "I hardly remember most of it. I was just so lucky not to have found myself pregnant."

He scowled. "The boy didn't use protection?"

"I was too drunk to notice."

"But surely—" His jaw clenched, then he forced himself to relax. "I'll make a deal with you. We'll make love, but if at any time you want me to stop, I will."

Her throat convulsed. "You'd do that?"

Something softened inside him. "I want a willing female in my bed. I don't get my kicks from forcing a woman." Rising, he held out his hand. "I need you. Need to make love with you, Kia Benton," he said, deliberately saying her name, wanting her to know that he knew exactly who she was, unlike the boy who had stripped her of her virginity. "I promise you this won't be like your first time."

Seven

The evening breeze gently lifted the lace curtains away from the open window as Kia followed Brant into the bedroom. In a way, she felt like those curtains. As if she was lifting a part of herself, unveiling herself for him to see.

Yet it was a risky move to make, and for a moment she hesitated. Did she really want him to leap the boundaries she kept around herself? Today in his office she'd relinquished her body to him. But now, once his body was inside her, once he knew her so physically, what would happen to her emotionally?

Just then, he squeezed her fingers and she looked at him. The sheer depth of desire in his eyes made her shiver with longing. All her doubts disappeared.

"I want you, Brant," she admitted, unable to stop the words from spilling from her. She couldn't deny herself this. No matter what happened afterward, no matter what he thought of her, she would always have this memory. "I want you so much."

Heat flared in his eyes. "Then you've got me," he muttered, pulling her close.

She went willingly into his arms, the palms of her hands pressing against his chest, feeling his warmth and vibrancy through the material of his shirt.

"I have *never* had a more beautiful woman in my arms," he rasped, his warm breath flowing over her.

"You make me *feel* beautiful," she murmured. And he did. As if someone had waved a magic wand over her and turned her into more than she was.

She lifted her face for his kiss, and his mouth swept down and took possession of hers. And from that moment on she was his. Her need had been smoldering inside her for so long now. She needed this release.

His mouth moved against hers, silently telling her how much he wanted her. She reveled in it, opening her lips, letting him take whatever he wanted yet returning the favor. She wanted to be a part of him, so much a part of him that he'd never forget her.

The kiss deepened, lengthened. His hands caressed her spine through her dress, then eased down the zipper to stroke her bare skin, gliding up to the curve of her shoulders and provocatively pushing the material aside like a maestro playing their song.

He broke off the kiss and skimmed his lips along her jaw. Hypnotized by his touch, she arched her neck, as his mouth continued to her earlobe and then proceeded down the smooth column of her throat. He planted a tantalizing kiss at the hollow of her neck and she gave a soft moan and slid her hands beneath the material of his shirt, not prepared to wait another millisecond to touch him.

Her head spun at the first feel of his warm flesh beneath her tingling palms. "Oh, my God," she whispered, the shock of his taut muscles running through her body even as she luxuriated in feeling the strong beat of his heart against her palms. Strong and fast.

"You're playing with fire," he said, shuddering, then stormed her mouth again in a kiss that sent her up in flames. At the same time he clasped her hips, grounding her against him. She'd felt his arousal once before when they'd danced together. This was different. This was her first full contact of him as a man. It stunned her. Delighted her. It made her ache for him.

He pulled away and in one swift motion tugged at her dress, letting it rush down her body and fall to the floor. But he didn't stop to stare, though she felt his gaze on her. Her bra vanished next. Her panties followed. Then he swept her up in his arms and carried her over to the bed, laying her out on top of the comforter.

And that's when he finally stopped to look down upon her. The intensity in his eyes sang through her veins, making her very much aware of being not only a woman but the woman he wanted.

"Tonight you're mine, Kia."

Her throat went dry. She wanted to deny it, but how could she deny something so intrinsically right?

"Yes," she whispered.

His hands went to his shirt and he quickly began to undress. It hit the carpet, followed by his trousers. It didn't take long before he stood beside her all naked and in full glory.

Her breath caught in her throat. He was absolutely magnificent, with a beautifully proportioned body that shot her pulse right off the chart. His broad shoulders topped a powerful chest that fostered wisps of dark hair and tapered down to lean hips and long, muscular legs. And to a commanding erection that magnified his masculinity tenfold.

He joined her on the bed and she surrendered to the moment, to herself, to him. She gasped when his lips moved to her breast and enclosed a nipple, pleasuring her into a mindless state even as his hand brushed over her hip and dipped to the junction at her thighs. His fingers slid between her feminine folds and ran around the small, sensitive nub in circles. Sanity began to blur as her world shrank to that one caress of his finger, to the sweet tug of his mouth at her breast.

But then, just as she was about to go over the edge, he pulled away, making her cry out in intense disappointment. "Don't stop!"

"Shh. This time we make love together," he murmured, reaching for a foil packet on the bedside table. He sheathed himself and poised at her thighs. She softened beneath him, ready to take him into her. *Needing* him in her.

"Open yourself to me," he said, nudging her legs farther apart, and she did willingly.

He entered her slowly, his eyes never leaving her face as her tightness confirmed what she had told him earlier. No *man* had ever filled her in this way before. Acknowledging this, his eyes bathed her with a tenderness that took her breath away. Then he filled her completely, gently, only stopping when he could fill her no more. His sensitivity made her heart roll over.

For one long moment they stayed still, each studying the other, connected in both body and spirit. It was the most profound moment Kia had ever experienced. She sensed it was the same for him.

As if in silent agreement, he took a deep breath and slowly began to withdraw. Then he moved forward and filled her again. He took another breath and withdrew as far as he could without separating their bodies. He kept repeating the motion, and she lifted her hips to take more of him into her, feeling something building, something so electric she had to close her eyes.

"Look at me," he said hoarsely, and she moaned but she did what he told her, finding it incredibly erotic when he mesmerized her with his eyes and began to move once more. He picked up the pace, and that rush of heat turned into a whipcord of male muscle, stamping her with each thrust of his body, taking everything she had within her. She offered it up to the one man in the world worthy of everything she had to give.

"Brant!" she cried as he rasped out her name

in a strangled tone that said he couldn't hold on much longer either. He kissed her then. A deep, deep kiss that was followed by a final plummet of his body as she arched against him.

They reached their climax together, holding themselves as one, in total sync at this precious moment in time.

Kia spiraled down to a hazy aftermath with a series of lingering kisses before he rolled over and held her in his arms for a few moments.

Then she watched his long, lean length disappear, as he rose and headed toward the bathroom. She lay back and closed her eyes. She had to, otherwise when he came back he would see something that had just hit her.

She had fallen in love with him.

Shock ran through her. She went hot, then cold. *She loved Brant Matthews.* She would love him until the day she died, even knowing she would never be enough for him. Dear God, this couldn't be…yet she knew it was, felt it in her heart.

The bed sank on one side and she scarcely dared to breathe. Brant was sitting beside her, waiting for her to look at him.

"Kia?" he murmured, tenderly pushing some strands of hair from her face.

She had no alternative but to look at him and pray that he didn't see what was so obvious to her now. How had she not seen this coming?

Her eyelids lifted, and her breath hitched in her throat at the look in his eyes. It was all-knowing. All male. Full of sexual satisfaction.

And he had no idea she loved him.

Thank God. She could breathe easier now and enjoy their time together. That's all she'd let herself ask for. That's all she'd let herself want. It would be over soon enough. And if he ran true to form—as her father did with his women friends—having gotten what he'd wanted from her, she wouldn't be seeing much more of him after this anyway. She shivered. Already that thought cut through her heart.

"Did I hurt you?" he murmured.

"No." But he would. When he dumped her.

His shoulders relaxed, his mouth curving with sheer sensuality. "Woman, that was the best sex I've ever had."

Yes, that's all it came down to with Brant. She tried not to show her hurt. "Me, too."

"For all intents and purposes, you were a virgin." He leaned forward and gave her a long, slow kiss, then looked into her eyes. "I'm honored I was the first *man* to sleep with you." He kissed her again briefly, then leaned back, an odd look in his eyes. "Why?"

Her breath stopped and she realized he saw more than she'd thought. She licked her lips. "Because I...I mean, you..." She shrugged. "Well, what woman wouldn't want to make love with you?"

His mouth twisted. "Flattery will get you everywhere," he mocked, but she had the feeling he wasn't happy with her answer.

But if he expected a declaration of love, he was going to be disappointed. Maybe that's what his other women always provided, but she wasn't about to copy them. She swallowed hard at the thought of all those other women who would come after her. She couldn't bear to think about it. And she wasn't going to wait around for him to throw her away like some piece of garbage that was past its use-by date either.

Panicking, she sat up, almost knocking him out of the way. He put his hands on her shoulders, stilling her.

"What's the matter?" he said with a scowl.

"I'm going home." She tried to push him away, but he kept his body firmly in front of her.

Surprise came and went in his eyes before they flared with anger. "I won't let you run out on me, Kia."

"*You* won't let *me?*" she choked out. Did he think because he'd made her his own she would leave her brains at the door?

"I've already had one woman who mattered run out on me. I'm not going to let you do the same. Not yet, anyway."

She gave a soft gasp. A woman *who mattered* had run out on him? And she was in the same category? But what did he mean by mattered?

"Are you saying that I'm…that we…?" She tried to find the words to say it. "Is there something more between us than I think, Brant?"

He stood up, and she saw he had wrapped a white towel around his lower half. "You bet there's something between us. And we're going to see it through to the end."

The end. She shouldn't be surprised by his choice of words, yet she was. How could she love this devil of a man? Fate had certainly played a sick joke on her.

"Don't tell me what to do, Brant."

"If I told you everything I wanted you to do, you'd run for your life."

She got to her feet, wrapping the sheet

around her as she did. "I don't need to run. I'm leaving anyway."

"I don't think so," he warned ominously.

Her heart jumped in her chest. "You can't stop me."

Can't I? his eyes said arrogantly. "Then you have nothing to lose by coming over here and kissing me like you mean it. Do that, and I'll even hold the door open for you on the way out."

She moistened her suddenly dry lips. "And if I don't?"

"Then I'll come over there and kiss you, and we'll see where it leads."

"What a choice," she muttered.

She swallowed. One kiss. Could she kiss him this one time and get away with it? She knew she would melt in his arms again. She knew she would want more. But hadn't she always prided herself on her strength of will?

Without stopping to think further, she pulled the sheet tighter and closed the distance between them. Then she went up on her toes and quickly kissed him on the mouth before turning away.

He grabbed her arm and spun her back toward him, his eyes holding a faint glint of humor. "Like you mean it, I said."

Somehow she'd known he wouldn't let her get away with that chaste peck. "Oh, but I did mean it like that," she mocked, even as a thrill raced through her. This time she'd give him exactly what he wanted and more. Then she'd walk out that door, put everything back on a business level and hope to God she could cope with knowing she'd fallen in love with a man who thought *woman* was a synonym for *sex*.

Her heart beating at full speed, she moved back toward him. In the split second before she put her lips to his, she saw his eyes darken and she realized she'd never once instigated a kiss with him. The other two Christmas kisses had been him coming to her, not the other way around. She felt thrillingly provocative.

She placed her mouth to his and began a kiss that gave him all the love she had inside her. Her stomach quivered even as she let her tongue slide around his mouth, then briefly dip between his slightly parted lips. She heard his groan deep within his throat, so she repeated the action, this time her tongue sliding over the top of his, tasting him, loving him.

The clean male scent of him exuded an attraction she found difficult to deny, and her arms slid up around his neck and cupped the back of his head, holding him to her, deepening the kiss. The sheet slipped down between them, and she felt the muscles of his chest tighten against her bare breasts. She rubbed herself against him, the feel of curly male hair teasing her nipples.

Suddenly he broke off the kiss with a guttural sound that made her think he had almost reached his limit. Then he swung her up in his arms and strode toward the bathroom.

"You're heading the wrong way," she murmured, not really caring right now that she was supposed to be leaving and not coming back.

"No, I'm not. I know exactly where we're going."

They made leisurely love in the spa surrounded by tropical plants that gave a dreamy quality to the setting. Kia responded to Brant's instructions and sat on his lap facing him, with him inside her. It was an incredible experience. And the most brave. Face-to-face like that, she had to stop herself from crying out she loved him.

Then they made their way back to the bed, and she reveled in taking her time to explore his male body before he growled her name, rolled on top of her and made love to her all over again. Exhausted, they fell into a deep sleep.

The ringing of the telephone next to the bed woke them during the night. Kia groaned and pressed her cheek against Brant's bare chest, wanting to hold on to the euphoria, hoping the noise would go away so she could go back to sleep.

Vaguely she was aware of Brant reaching out an arm to pick it up. She heard the deep rumble of his voice as he answered it. Then, the next thing she knew, he'd jerked into a sitting position, throwing her off him.

"What the hell?" she heard him say as she lay on her back and came fully awake. "My God! Julia?"

There was silence for a moment as the person on the other end of the phone responded. Then Brant's gaze skidded to Kia and darkened. "Yes, I have company," he answered in clipped tones. He listened. "Now?" He looked at Kia again, then away. "Okay. Give me half an hour." He hung up and turned back to her. "I've got to go out for a while. Something's come up."

Yes, and her name is Julia.

"Don't worry, I understand. Totally."

His face hardened as he swung his legs over the side of the bed. "I didn't ask for your understanding."

That hurt. "Aren't you lucky I gave it anyway?" she snapped, throwing back the bedclothes.

"You don't have to leave."

Did he think she would wait for him to go to this woman, then come back to bed and make love to *her?*

"I don't want to stay."

A long moment crept by as she gathered her clothes from the floor.

"Then I'll walk you down to your car."

"Don't bother." She looked up and caught his eyes going hungrily over her naked body. A quiver surged through her veins and she wondered if she could stop him going to this Julia.

Then she realized what she was thinking and her lips tightened. Did she really want to compete with another woman? No, she'd had enough of watching her mother fight for her father's love.

Brant pulled on his trousers. "Nevertheless, I insist. It's late."

Yes, far too late, she thought, glancing at the clock and seeing it was two in the morning. It had been a mistake to make love to him. A beautiful mistake at the time but a mistake nevertheless.

In a damning silence they finished dressing, then he walked down with her to the underground car park.

"Call me as soon as you get home," he ordered, holding the car door open for her. "Use my cell phone number. I want to know you're safe."

She squashed the spark of warmth at his

concern. He was only protecting what he thought was temporarily his. "I'll be fine."

"Call me," he warned, his dark gaze holding hers. "If you don't, I'll call you."

She didn't respond as she started the engine and drove out of the car park without looking back. Which is exactly what she'd have to do where he was concerned anyway. Walk away and not look back.

She was halfway home when something occurred to her. Was this Julia the woman who had "mattered"? Without a doubt she knew that she was. And obviously Julia *still* mattered or Brant would still be in bed with *her* right now.

Kia didn't call him when she got home. Worse, he didn't call her, and that made her heart sink more. Obviously she wasn't as important to him as Julia.

Kia got no sleep for the rest of the night and by morning she felt exhausted. Not even her usual shower, followed by a breakfast of sliced mango, nor a cup of coffee, could make her feel the slightest bit better.

If only she didn't love Brant. It would all be so much easier if he was the kind of man she thought might eventually love her in return. Only he wasn't. And he never would be. A leopard didn't change its spots. A womanizer didn't become trustworthy. The word *faithful* wasn't in his dictionary.

Phillip rang as she headed out the door. She'd decided to go to work early and get some of the paperwork typed and on Brant's desk before he came in. He was bound to be late, if he turned up at all.

"What do you think you're doing sending some woman to seduce me?" Phillip joked, his tone so heartbreakingly light that Kia had to smile.

"And did Lynette succeed?"

"Let's just say she surpassed all expectations." There was a slight hesitation. "How can we ever thank you for all you've done, Kia?" he said softly.

"Just be happy. That's all the thanks I want."

"We will. And we want you to come to the wedding in two months time. We would have scheduled it earlier, but I have to see one more doctor, then I'm all hers."

Kia knew she wouldn't want to go to the wedding. How could she bear seeing Brant in a social situation? Worse, with Julia by his side.

"I'll put it in my calendar."

"Speaking of calendars, aren't you supposed to be spending Christmas with your family in Adelaide? Lynette told me you were in the office yesterday."

She tried to think quickly without worrying him. "I did spend Christmas at home, but I got away early." She gave a light laugh. "Too much noise. Too many people. You know how holidays are."

"But you didn't have to go back to work so soon." He paused. "Or is there a problem at the office I'm not aware of?"

"No, of course not," she assured him quickly. "I just popped in yesterday to pick up something I'd left behind, and Brant was there and needed something typed so I stayed."

A moment's silence, then he said, "Remind me to give you a bonus. Of course, most women think working with Brant would be bonus enough...." He trailed off suggestively.

"No doubt."

"I'll have to tell him, you know. About me and Lynette." He sounded worried. "You'll be open season after that."

She pretended to be unconcerned. "He already knows. He overheard Lynette and I talking yesterday."

"And?"

"And nothing." Time to go. "Phillip, I have an appointment and I'm running late."

"Oh, damn. I've just realized something. Word's bound to get out about you and I breaking up." He swore. "And I can't get back there just yet to help you."

"I'll manage." Phillip's idea of helping would probably make the situation worse anyway.

"But you're going to bear the brunt of it, Kia. Some people might think you dumped me because of my limp," he reminded her.

She pushed aside thoughts of what that journalist would say and knew there was only one answer. "Not if we're honest with them." Holding back the truth from everyone was of little value now anyway. "It's the best way to go."

He drew in a long breath. "Yes, you're right."

"Look, I really must be going."

"Kia?"

She stiffened. "Yes?"

"Are you sure you're okay?"

"Of course I am, Phillip. Thanks for asking. I'll talk to you soon." She quickly hung up so he wouldn't hear the catch in her voice. She couldn't bear that anyone else knew her feelings for Brant. As far as she was concerned, loving Brant was something so private, so personal, she couldn't share it with another soul.

Eight

Kia stepped out of the elevator at ten past eight and was tempted to tiptoe to her office just in case Brant was at his desk. But that would be acting like a coward, she decided, straightening her shoulders and striding down the hallway. The empty offices were quiet.

She reached Brant's door and glanced inside, her throat aching with defeat when she saw the room empty. Had she really thought he'd be at work? Dear God, how could he make love to her last night, then go to another woman? Her heart squeezed in anguish. It was morally wrong. So why was she surprised? Just because she loved him didn't change what he was.

Swallowing hard, she forced herself to continue to her office. She was beginning to have a new appreciation for the turmoil her mother had gone through with her father. She loved her mother dearly, but she'd never really understood how a woman could stay with a man who cared for her so little. She'd even sometimes thought of her mother as weak when it came to her father. Now she knew it had taken a special kind of blind loyalty to stay with him as long as she had.

An hour later Kia stretched, rose from her desk and went to stand at the window. She looked down at the sun-shadowed street below. The world continued to turn, but inside she felt dead, as if her heart had shriveled into a rock. She had to forget Brant, but she couldn't even summon the energy to do that right now. He still hadn't arrived. He was still with—

"Kia?"

She spun toward the sound. The heart she thought dead leaped to life. Brant stood in the doorway, dressed in a fresh set of clothes that made him look clean and vital and so disturbingly handsome that her knees turned weak.

She lifted her gaze to find him watching her with a knowing intensity that made heat surge into her cheeks. His look said she couldn't hide from him. That she was *his*.

Then reality kicked in and her stomach clenched tight. Physical closeness wasn't enough. It would never be enough. Her feelings for him ran too deep.

"I didn't think you'd be here so early," she said coolly, determined to keep her distance.

His eyes narrowed. "Why not?"

"I thought you'd be…preoccupied."

He started to close the gap between them.

"Preoccupied with what?" he said silkily. "Or should I say *whom?*"

She managed a shrug. "With Julia, of course."

He stopped right in front of her. "Ah…you mean *in bed* with Julia, don't you?"

Did he have to rub it in? Was he getting some masochistic pleasure from pointing this out?

Her chin lifted. "Look, if you want to sleep with other women, that's fine. Just don't expect me to like it. Or to accept it. I won't share any man." She saw something flare in his eyes. "Julia's welcome to you," she ended in disgust.

There was a lethal calmness in his eyes. "So you're telling me to choose between you and Julia?"

"No, I'm telling you to choose between me and any other women you want to sleep with, *including* Julia."

"I don't take kindly to ultimatums. And I don't explain my actions to anyone." His arrogant gaze slid over her, pausing a moment on the swell of her breasts. "But for you, dear Kia, I'm going to relent on that last one. I did *not* sleep with Julia last night. The only woman I slept with was you, and then we got very little sleep, as I recall."

She wanted to believe him. Oh, how she wanted to. But how could she forget those nights listening to her mother's hushed accusations and her father's denials. Denials that had always proven to be lies.

She met his gaze with steely-eyed determination. "Very clever, Brant, but unlike some women, I don't believe everything I'm told. You say you didn't *sleep* with Julia. But you didn't deny having sex with her."

A shadow of anger swept across his face. "That's because I *didn't* have sex with her."

"I've heard *that* one before," she said, turning away.

He grabbed her by the shoulder and spun her back. "Listen. I am *not* your father."

She sucked in a sharp breath, stunned by his perceptiveness. Was she so transparent? Or did she subconsciously wear her thoughts blazoned across her back?

His hold tightened. "Kia, you once said you wouldn't apologize for him. Well, I'm not going to apologize for him either. Your father is a shallow man without integrity. Do you really think I'm like him?"

Her mind reeled in confusion. She'd never even considered the possibility that he *wasn't* like her father.

His jaw clenched. "You either believe me or you don't. It's your decision."

She stared up at him, trying to assess if he was telling the truth. If he was, then she'd have to reverse her opinion of him. That wasn't an easy thing to do.

She saw the strain in his eyes and etched around his nose and mouth. Suddenly she knew that if she didn't believe him, then it would be the end of them. He would shut her out of his life for good without a single regret.

And it was *that* very thing that made her admit he had a deep sense of personal integrity, unlike her father. She just hadn't let herself see it until now.

"I believe you," she said softly but firmly.

His chest rose and fell, but it was the flash of relief in his eyes that made her heart constrict. It overwhelmed her to know he really cared what she thought of him.

His fingers loosened on her shoulders. "Thank you," he said with a casual sort of dignity that was at odds with the arrogance just beneath the surface.

All at once she knew this was no longer just about her believing Brant.

"And now you've got to believe something about *me*," she said, taking this chance, knowing this was important to her. "I'm telling you truthfully that I'm *not* a gold digger, I've never worked anyone to get either money or marriage out of them and I'm not with *you* for money or marriage." She lifted her chin with clear determination, her heart slamming against her ribs. "You can choose to believe me or not."

He studied her face for more than one heart-beat, his eyes not leaving hers for a second, but she saw the jolt of surprise in them, the assessment of her words, a decision and finally the admiration.

"I believe you," he murmured, pulling her into his arms, holding her close, which was just as well because her knees had given way. The knowledge that he was seeing her as the person she was for the first time made her feel gloriously thankful.

He leaned back. "And for the record, just in case you think you're like your mother because you believe me like she did with your father, you're *not*. So you have no need to feel guilty."

She frowned. "Guilty?"

The sensual spread of his mouth made her heart hammer against her ribs. "For wanting me."

Her frown disappeared as her lips began to twitch. "Who said I wanted you?"

"I seem to remember a few whispered pleas in my ears last night," he murmured, lifting her hands and placing them around his neck. She didn't resist.

"Hey, that was me begging you to let me sleep."

"Oh, really? Perhaps we should repeat it tonight and see." His warm breath caressed her cheeks.

"Not tonight," she teased. "I'm busy."

"You'd better not have a date," he growled.

"I want to wash my hair."

"I'll wash it for you."

"Will you do my ironing, too?"

He chuckled and pulled her closer. "We can come to a compromise. Wear non-crushable clothes. Better yet, wear no clothes at all. It'll make for a very interesting evening."

Just the thought of how interesting it could be made her feel very sexy. "My place or yours?" she asked throatily, amazed at how easily she'd slipped into the role of seductress.

"Mine," he murmured, nuzzling her neck. Then he gave her a quick, hard kiss and let her go. "I've got a meeting in an hour with one of the Anderson executives. We'll continue this tonight. I'll pick you up at seven."

She was melting so fast she had to keep some independence. "I can drive myself."

"Fine, but don't plan on leaving early." He gave her a smile that sent her pulse spinning. "In fact, I doubt I'll let you leave at all."

At seven-fifteen Kia found herself once again standing in front of Brant's penthouse. It was hard to believe she'd been here twenty-four hours ago, and even then she'd sworn to herself it was a one-off thing. Talk about making the same mistake twice. Talk about being a woman weakened by love.

When he opened the door, it was like opening the door to her heart. Everything inside her reached for him, enveloped him, made him hers. It was the oddest feeling, yet it felt so right.

He didn't say a word. He just stepped back and let her pass, then kicked the door shut with his foot, his hand sliding around her arm and turning her to face him. She had no idea how long they stood gazing at each other.

"Come here," he finally murmured and tugged her toward him. She went willingly, and his lips found hers, and she simply gave herself up to him and his touch. He made her feel whole. As if her world had been split in two until this moment and now the top and bottom half of her heart had been sealed with love. Her love for him.

Overwhelmed with emotion, wanting him, needing to touch him, she broke off the kiss and began undoing the buttons on his shirt, stripping it from his broad torso as he stood and watched her with a look in his eyes that seared through to her soul.

"Too much," she whispered, not just about him standing in front of her but about her feelings for him.

"Yes," he said brusquely, watching her as she placed her hands on his hair-roughened chest. She skimmed her palms over him and heard him groan, loving the feel of him and the scent of him. She inhaled deeply against his skin.

In one smooth motion she reached for his trousers and pulled down the zipper, freeing him. His erection was all male and challenged her to touch him more. He rasped her name as her hand slithered around him and gripped him, moving over his hard flesh, rousing his passion, rousing her own even more.

"Not yet," he muttered, grabbing her hand and moving her back from him. Then he stripped the clothes from her body with a quickness and hunger that astounded her before swinging her up in his arms and carrying her to bed, where he lay her down, then sheathed himself.

In one quick motion he entered her. And just like that she came. No slow crawl toward orgasm. No indulgent inching to reach the pinnacle of pleasure. Just a powerful, all-ful-filling climax that made her shudder and cry out his name.

And when she caught her breath, he was looking down at her with another one of those arrogantly satisfied looks on his face that somehow didn't offend her this time. It made her feel very womanly.

And in a womanly way, she lifted her body slightly, nudging him farther into her.

"Too much," he growled, repeating her

words, and he began to move. Slow at first, then faster and faster, the muscles in his neck growing taut with strain. He allowed her to have one more glorious climax before groaning her name and plunging deeper into her, burning them both in a downpour of fiery sensation.

It was a long, long moment before either of them could breathe, let alone move. Brant was the first to stir, and all at once Kia didn't want him to leave her. She wanted to stay right here, like this, forever. She tightened her arms around his back and held him close against her. She heard the rumble of his voice, but her fingers couldn't seem to unlock themselves.

"Kia?" he repeated, giving a low, masculine laugh against her neck. "As much as I love being inside you, you've got to let me go sometime."

His words finally penetrated. Her fingers loosened. He was right. She was making a fool of herself.

He lifted his upper body away from her, his

eyes sexily amused yet strangely serious. "What was that all about?"

She forced a slight smile. "Just faint with hunger. I haven't eaten much today," she admitted. She'd been too nervous to eat.

"Then you need food, woman," he teased. He gave her one brief, hard kiss, rolled off her and headed to the bathroom. She hardly had time to think before he was back carrying a white bathrobe.

"Here," he said, tossing the robe toward her, his gaze sweeping over her naked body with male appreciation before he disappeared.

She could get used to this, she decided as she stood up and wrapped herself in the fluffy material, enjoying its warmth in the air-conditioned apartment, burying herself in its male scent.

Her eyes widened as he came back into the room wearing nothing but a pair of well-pressed jeans. Jeans, for heaven's sake. Brant

Matthews in jeans? And black ones at that. Normally he dressed as the consummate businessman. In jeans he looked what he was—the ultimate female fantasy.

He caught her staring and his eyes smoldered back in return. "If you want me on the main menu, you only have to say so."

A delicious shudder heated her body. "Actually, I think I'd like to keep you for dessert."

"That can be arranged."

They ate dinner in the small, intimate dining room. Or perhaps it seemed intimate because of the casual way they were dressed—her in his bathrobe, him in jeans.

Or maybe it was the look in his eyes. She tried to keep her cool, but that knowing look heated her cheeks and made her want to follow him like a lamb back into the bedroom.

Suddenly panicked by her loss of willpower, she said the first thing that came to mind. "Tell me about Julia," she heard herself say, then bit back a groan of dismay, not meaning to bring up the other woman again.

Or had she? Julia still played on her mind. Oh, not because she believed Brant was having an affair with her any longer, but there was something there, something still not quite right.

His eyes hardened as he put his coffee cup down. "She's my sister-in-law."

"Your what! Why didn't you tell me? Why did you let me believe she was—"

"One of my women?" His mouth tightened. "She *was* one of my women. Then she ran off to marry my brother."

"What! Oh, Brant, I'm so sorry."

"Don't be. It ended up for the best."

She frowned, not so sure he really believed that. It obviously wasn't for the best that a woman who had mattered had left him for the one person in the world he should have been able to trust, his brother. He wouldn't be bitter about it otherwise.

"So why is she contacting you now?" she asked, almost afraid to hear the answer. Did the other woman want Brant back? Is this what all this was about?

His piercing blue eyes contrasted sharply with the shrug he gave. "She wants help with Royce. He can't handle the fact that Julia and I were once an item and he's developed a drinking problem over it. Julia asked me to speak to him and make him see sense."

A swell of relief filled her. "Did you?"

"No."

She stared at him in astonishment. "He's your brother, Brant."

"I know."

A shiver skittered under her skin. "Surely that means something?"

"Does it?"

This, more than anything, showed her exactly how he would treat her when the time came. And come it would. When he tired of her.

Dear God, it stunned her to know how much she'd been fooling herself. Just because she'd admitted Brant had more integrity than her father didn't mean he'd suddenly turned into Mr. Nice Guy. When he wanted her out of his life, he'd take the appropriate measures to do exactly that. No exceptions.

Well, maybe one.

Julia.

"You're a coldhearted bastard," she muttered, her heart twisting painfully inside her.

His eyes turned as unreadable as stone. "Feel free to think what you like."

"Oh, I will," she said, holding his gaze, determined he knew she didn't appreciate this side of his character.

For a moment silence hung angrily in the air.

Then he said, "Tell me one thing, Kia. Do you think if you went to your father right now and told him how you feel about him, it would change the way he thinks?"

She frowned. "What's my father got to do with this?"

"You're asking *me* to go to my brother and change his mind. It's a similar situation. And it won't work."

"But how do you know unless you try?"

His eyes bored into her. "Did you try with your father?"

She blinked in surprise. "Yes, I did."

"And what happened?"

She blanched, remembering. "He wouldn't listen."

"Exactly."

She sighed. Brant had a point.

His eyes softened. "Look, my uncle was an alcoholic. It ruined his family even before he killed himself and my aunt in a car accident while he was driving drunk. So don't you see? I *know* I can talk until I'm blue in the face and it won't change how my brother feels. I *know*

I can get his promise that he'll get help, and tomorrow he'll break it. No, he has to want to seek help for himself. Not expect his wife to fix it for him. Or me."

Kia heard the rough edge of emotion in his voice and knew he wasn't as cold as he made out. "You're right."

He stood and pulled her up into his arms, his eyes darkening. "I don't want to argue anymore. I want to make love to you. Let's forget the rest of the world tonight."

"But—"

"Enough," he murmured, undoing her belt to slide his hands inside the robe and over the bare skin of her hips.

Hypnotized by his touch, she tingled under his fingertips. Greedily she gave herself up to him and to whatever he wanted to do to her.

"You need another lesson in some loving, Ms. Benton," he said, nuzzling her neck beneath the collar of her bathrobe.

She gasped with delight as his hands slid up her rib cage and cupped her breasts.

He leaned back. "Good. That's lesson number one completed."

Her breath caught in her throat as he squeezed her nipples, his touch sending shock waves to every nerve center in her body. "Er… number one?"

"Always respond when I touch you."

That was easy. "What's…number two?"

"Always say my name when I'm inside you."

She moaned as his hands slid up to her shoulders. "And if I don't?"

"Then we start over until you do," he murmured, pushing the robe off her shoulders and letting it fall to the carpet.

She licked her lips. "I was always a quick learner."

His eyes devoured her. "That's too bad."

"Why?"

"I was looking forward to teaching you the next lesson," he said huskily.

Her body was heavy with warmth. "Um… next lesson?"

"Lesson number three. How to get a man to kiss you all over."

She shuddered. And suddenly she wanted to know what *he* tasted like. What he would feel like against her tongue. "Do I get to reciprocate?"

His eyes darkened dangerously. "Only if you want to."

"Oh, I do."

"Then that'll be lesson number four," he murmured, rubbing a thumb across her lips.

"When do we start, teacher?"

"Now is as good a time as any," he drawled and pulled her closer.

Her mouth parted the instant his lips met hers and he kissed her with a hunger that shocked her. It was as if it had been years since they'd been together instead of a mere half hour.

He kissed a path down to her breasts, anointing each one with his mouth before going down on his knees and kissing her intimately through the curls at her thighs. His tongue flicked over the hot, moist core of her, and she gasped his name out loud, grasping his head to her as his tongue did marvelous things to her over-sensitized body.

"Come inside me," she implored, her hands pulling at his head to make him stop before she spilled over the edge. "Please, Brant."

He paused briefly. "Soon," he promised and returned to what he was doing, making her legs weaken as she melted around him, shuddering with intensity, suspended in time.

When he swung her up in his arms and carried her into the shower, her brain felt clouded, her body thoroughly seduced. He kissed her back to life and then led her into the bedroom.

"I want to please you like you pleased me, Brant," she murmured, following him down on the bed.

His eyes smoldered. "Are you sure you're ready?"

"Absolutely."

So he told her in explicit terms how a man liked to be made love to. She didn't need much encouragement as she kissed his chest, letting her mouth move all over him, and downward through the arrow of hair on his taut stomach, until she covered the tip of his erection with her lips.

"Kia," he growled her name as she began her own lesson in loving that had nothing to do with experience and everything to do with womanly instinct. She wanted him. *All* of him. And she almost got it.

Until he pulled her head up and away from him with a growl. "No," he muttered tightly, twisting to reach a condom on the bedside table. A few seconds later he rolled her beneath him and plunged inside her in one swift motion, quickly reigniting the fuse of desire inside her, plunging deeper and deeper until both of them shattered together in a sea of sensual pleasure.

Afterward she lay with her cheek resting against his chest. She had to ask, "Why, Brant? I wanted to."

He kissed the top of her head. "I know, but you weren't ready to take such a step, as good as you were."

"But…"

"Sweetheart, let me be the judge of that," he murmured sleepily.

Kia tilted her head back to look at the angular contours of his face. She loved the inherent strength in his features. That firm thrust of his jaw. Those undeniable lips. But she had to wonder exactly *who* wasn't ready for a full sexual commitment. The man who knew the score? Or the woman who supposedly didn't?

* * *

Brant waited for Kia's soft breath to tell him she was asleep before he opened his eyes and looked down at her naked body entwined with his. She was so beautiful. So bloody gorgeous.

And she was the only woman he hadn't let "go all the way." He wasn't sure why, but he did know he couldn't let her do what other women had done for him. Maybe because she'd asked first instead of taken. No other woman had ever asked. Not even Julia.

Not that it wouldn't have given him pleasure. It would have. Intense pleasure. But being with Kia wasn't about mere physical pleasure anymore. Deep down he'd known that all along but today when she'd stood her ground, forced him to admit she wasn't the gold digger he thought she was, something inside his chest had shifted. He just hadn't realized how profoundly she touched him. Yet it wasn't love.

No, never that. He'd had one kick in the guts from a woman. He'd never let that happen again. Not even if she asked.

Nine

The next morning the telephone rang as soon as Kia stepped inside her house. Thinking it was Brant calling to tease her why she was late for work, she laughed softly and raced to answer it on legs that almost flew across the living room. For the first time she felt almost happy to be in love.

"How's my beautiful girl then?" a booming male voice came down the line.

The animation died on her face. Dear God, why did her father have to call now?

She forced herself to relax. "Hello, Dad."

"You sound disappointed. Not expecting anyone else to call, were you? One of your many boyfriends, no doubt."

"I've never been one for many boyfriends," she said as calmly as she could. She wasn't like *him.* She didn't need adoration every minute of the day.

"A man friend then. Is it serious?"

"How are things, Dad?" Her feelings for Brant were private.

He chuckled. "That's my darling girl. Don't tie yourself down until you're at least thirty. Until then, have a good time. A really good time, if you know what I mean."

"Oh, I will." Kia's heart ached. Her father had really sunk to a new low.

"Anyway," he continued. "I'm in Darwin for a couple of days on business and I thought we might have brunch together today."

"Brunch?"

"Yeah. I want to see if you're still as charming as ever."

"And if I'm not?" she quipped to hide her hurt.

"Then I'll trade you in," he joked and laughed out loud as if it was the funniest thing in the world.

Moisture filmed her eyes and she squeezed her eyelids shut. Thank heavens he couldn't see her.

"What do you say then, darling girl? Coming to see your old man for an early lunch?"

She blinked rapidly and took a deep breath. He didn't really care if he saw her or not, so she should tell him flat out no. Then it occurred to her—if she went, she could dispel any lingering doubts that Brant was like him. He really wasn't, she knew that, but why not take this opportunity to put it behind her once and for all?

"Will Amber be there?" she asked. It wouldn't be a pleasant lunch if the other woman attended. Not when her father's third wife was childishly jealous of her. Of course, Amber *was* half her father's age.

"No. I told her to stay in Sydney."

Kia's heart sank. So their marriage was on the rocks already. How sad. "Where and when?"

He named a restaurant in the heart of the city. She would have preferred to lunch at his hotel, but there was no chance of that. Her father liked to be seen when he was in town.

She laid the receiver on the cradle, then picked it up again, intending to call Brant and tell him why she wouldn't be in until later. Hearing his voice would be reassuring.

Then she remembered the invisible barrier he'd put up between them in bed last night and she stirred with sudden uneasiness. Perhaps it was best they both kept some distance.

Brant was just about to reach for the telephone for the tenth time when he heard the soft ping of the elevator door opening onto the executive floor.

Intense relief washed over him. It had to be Kia. Thank God nothing had happened to her. He'd already driven over to her place once this morning, to find out why she hadn't turned up at work after leaving his place earlier, and found no one at home. Her Porsche hadn't been in the driveway either. It had scared him silly, and that's something he didn't like to feel.

Bloody hell, he was going to demand an explanation, he decided, striding to the door, growing angry because she'd put him through this. He couldn't even think of an explanation that would satisfy him right now. Not unless...

His heart stopped, then began to thud like the deafening sound of tropical rain. Could she be seeing someone else? Was it possible so soon? Even Julia hadn't been quite that quick to run off with his brother.

With his gut tied up in knots, he reached the

door…only it wasn't Kia coming toward him. It was Flynn Donovan.

Brant swore.

"That's a nice way to greet an old friend," Flynn mocked as he approached.

Brant grimaced. "Sorry, mate. I wasn't swearing at you."

Flynn's dark brows lifted. "Then who?"

"It doesn't matter." He planted a wry smile on his face, trying to appear nonchalant. "This *is* an honor," he said, turning back into his office and going to stand in front of the window. He glanced down at the street below, hoping to see…

"Is it?"

Realizing his friend knew him too well and had astutely picked up on some of his anxiety, Brant spun around. "What are you doing here, Flynn?" he said, gesturing for him to sit on the leather couch.

But the other man remained standing, his finely tailored suit reflecting the successful businessman that he was, the watchful look in his eyes one that no doubt his competitors in the boardroom had seen many times. "I've come to ask why you haven't been returning my calls. I thought we were supposed to get together over Christmas."

Brant gave a short laugh. "That's a bit hard to do when you were in Japan and Damien was in the States."

"I was back for Christmas, and Damien will be here tomorrow. But that's not the point. The fact is you've been avoiding us."

Brant walked to his desk and dropped down on the chair. "I've been busy."

"Haven't we all?"

Brant silently swore to himself, not liking being under the microscope. It was okay when he got together with his friends and they ribbed each other mercilessly about other things, but this was about Kia, and she was no joke.

"Well, I've been extra busy." He decided to throw Flynn a crumb to satisfy him for now. "You remember how Phil had his accident?" Flynn gave a nod. "He almost lost us a major account. I've been working double time just to set things right."

A sharpening look from Flynn said he'd taken the bait. "Anything I can help you with?"

"Thanks, no. I've got it all under control now," he said, relaxing a little, then darted a look at the door when he thought he heard the sound of the elevator.

"You seem kind of jumpy," Flynn said, and Brant realized his friend hadn't been fooled at all.

He shrugged. "I'm just waiting for Phillip's PA to arrive."

"Kia Benton?"

Brant sucked in a lungful of air. "You know Kia?"

"No, but I saw her at a couple of functions with Phil. She's a stunner. I wouldn't mind dating her for a bit. No wonder Phil—"

"Shut it, Flynn!"

For a moment there was silence.

Then Flynn spoke. "What's she mean to you, Brant?"

"Nothing."

Flynn's lips twisted. "Come on, mate. I know when you're lying through your teeth."

"We're lovers."

Another moment's silence. Then Flynn said, "Does Phil know?"

"No, but he wouldn't be too concerned if he did." Brant briefly explained the part about Kia pretending to be Phillip's fiancée. He left out the bit about him thinking she was a gold digger, which was just as well. If she was playing him for a fool, she'd regret it, he vowed, swallowing a hard lump in his throat.

"So this is about you bedding a beautiful

woman because you thought she was out of reach and then she wasn't?"

"Yes."

Flynn gave a sardonic laugh. "Pull the other one, mate. I've known you all your life. There's more to you and Kia Benton than you're letting on. Am I right?"

Brant swore, hating being so obvious. "You're a son of a bitch," he said through half-gritted teeth.

"And how does she feel about you?" Flynn said, ignoring the tension coming out of his friend.

"How the hell do I know?"

"Perhaps you'd better do some fast talking or you might just find the lady will be snatched out from under you."

"Is that a threat?" Brant growled.

"Don't be stupid. All I'm saying is that she's a beautiful woman. She'd be a nice trophy for some men."

The thought of Kia being any man's trophy made him feel ill. "She wouldn't be interested."

"Really?" Flynn said in disbelief. "Let's see, a man could offer a woman like her riches beyond her imagination, travel across the globe, luxury like she's never seen before— and you're saying she wouldn't be interested? Get a grip, mate. Most women wouldn't be able to help themselves."

Brant stabbed his friend with his eyes, not appreciating having it spelled out like this. "When did you get to be so cynical?"

Flynn Donovan's eyes took on an odd glitter. "When I made my first million."

A couple of hours later Kia wondered how she'd ever thought Brant was like this man. The only thing the two men had in common was their gender. Brant may have a thing about commitment, but if he ever did fully commit to a woman, she knew it would be forever. And

Brant's children would know they were loved for who they were, not for what they looked like. Brant was nothing like Lloyd Benton. Thank God.

It was a relief to get away from her father. Now, more than ever, she appreciated loving Brant. It was a privilege to love him, even if he would soon break her heart.

So she was surprised and delighted to see the gray Mercedes parked out front of her house when she got home just after midday, needing to collect some papers before going into the office. She parked in the driveway, almost falling over herself getting out of the car and into his arms.

Only, after a couple of steps toward him, she realized something was wrong. Her steps faltered. A sick feeling rolled inside her stomach. "Brant?"

"Where have you been?" he said in an ominously low voice.

"Wh-what?"

"I came around two hours ago to look for you."

"You did?" Oh, how she would have preferred being with him.

His eyes hardened. "Where have you been all this time?"

She stiffened, her own anger beginning to mount. If he'd asked nicely, she would have answered nicely. As it was, she didn't like his possessive tone. Or the implication that she belonged to him. She wasn't even sure where this was coming from.

She sent him a glare even as she squashed a queasiness rising inside her. "I didn't realize I had to get your approval to go out."

His eyes impaled her. "If I'm being faithful to you, then you can bloody well be faithful to me."

She gasped. "Faithful? Who said anything about being *un*faithful?"

"If you've got nothing to hide, then why not just say where you've been?"

"It's the principle of the thing, Brant. You don't own me. I'm not your puppet to say and do what you please. You wouldn't like me if I was." Her lips twisted. "I'm a challenge, remember? Or I *was*."

His mouth tautened. "You still haven't told me where you've been."

"None of your damn bus—" All at once, nausea swelled in her throat. She felt clammy. Her head began to swirl. She grabbed hold of him to balance herself.

"Kia?" he said as if from a long way off. "What's the matter?"

"I feel…sick."

"Damn," he muttered, swinging her up in his arms. "Let's get you inside."

She wanted to tell him not to move too fast, but he seemed to sense that. He was surprisingly gentle as he carried her to the door and logged in the security code she managed to tell him before carrying her into the bedroom.

He went to lay her on the bed, but she motioned for him to take her into the bathroom instead. Somehow she found the strength to push him out of the room in case she lost her lunch. Luckily she didn't, and after a short while she began to feel a bit better.

After splashing water on her face, she looked up and jumped when she saw him standing there with a towel in his hand. Gratefully she accepted the cloth and began dabbing it against her cheeks.

His gaze went over her in concern. "Feeling better?"

"A little."

"Let's get you to bed."

She began to shiver. "I'm okay."

"Yeah, I can see that." He gave her a hand into the bedroom.

"You shouldn't have stayed," she mumbled as he helped her lay down on the bed.

"Why not?"

"I can take care of myself."

He covered her with a light blanket, but his look told her what he thought of that comment. "Rest. I'll be back in a minute." He left the room before she could ask where he was going.

A short time later she was back in the bathroom. And this time she *did* disgrace herself but was too sick to feel mortified with Brant's hands on her head, holding back her hair. When she'd finished, she rinsed her mouth, then he carried her back to bed, where she lay against the pillows.

She closed her eyes for a moment, and the next thing she knew was Brant gently shaking her awake. "Kia, wake up. The doctor's here."

She groaned and opened her eyes to find Brant and a strange middle-aged man standing beside her bed.

"How do you feel now, Ms. Benton?" the doctor asked.

She tried to sit up but fell back against the pillows. "Like my stomach's seasick."

"I'd better examine you." He glanced at Brant. "Perhaps you'd like to wait outside?"

"Perhaps not," Brant said, an inflexible look on his face that said he wasn't budging.

The doctor arched a brow at Kia. "Do you mind?"

Her eyes darted to Brant. It wouldn't matter if she did. "No."

"Right. Then let's take a look at you."

He examined her for a few minutes, then put his stethoscope away. "There's a stomach bug going around. I'd like to rule out food poisoning, though. Have you eaten anything today?"

"She had breakfast with me," Brant said before she could speak. "And I feel fine."

The doctor nodded. "That's good. What about lunch? Did you eat together?"

Brant's gaze stabbed her. "No."

Kia wanted to groan. There was no getting

around this. "I had something to eat in town," she said and saw Brant's shoulders tense.

The doctor frowned. "Hmm. Did you eat with anyone else? If you did, we'd better contact that other person and see if they're feeling okay. If they're not, we'll have to let the authorities know straightaway."

Kia glanced at Brant, who glared back in waiting silence. It was just as well she *wasn't* having an affair with anyone else. She'd be caught out otherwise. Not that she'd live to tell the tale.

"I had brunch with my father." She named the restaurant. "If you need to contact him, his cell phone number is written down near my phone."

"I'll call him now," Brant said, heading for the door, but not before she caught a glimpse of relief in his eyes. Her heart jolted painfully. He really *had* believed she was capable of an affair.

She was still mulling over that fact when he came back in the room.

"He's fine," he said, the unreadable look on his face telling Kia her father had been his usual irksome self but that Brant wasn't going to say anything about it to her. She swallowed a lump in her throat, suddenly overwhelmed by a strange feeling of relief. Brant truly didn't think any the less of her because of her father. In her heart, she hadn't been sure.

"Good," the doctor said, closing his medical bag with a snap. "I'll leave you something for the nausea."

"Thank you, Doctor," Brant said, then shortly after escorted the older man out of the bedroom.

A few minutes later he came back with a glass of water and a couple of the pills the doctor had given her. He helped her sit up while she took them, then laid her back against the pillows and tenderly pushed some blond strands of hair off her cheek.

Yet, oddly, his gesture brought to mind the time she had chicken pox and her father hadn't been able to hide his distaste at her appearance. Suddenly she felt self-conscious.

"I must look a mess," she said apologetically and tried to pat her hair in place.

He stared at her for a moment, then something flickered in the back of his eyes. "Never," he muttered, swinging away from her. He picked up the glass of water and took it into the bathroom.

Her heart jumped in her throat. She had the feeling he meant what he said. And if that were the case... No, she wouldn't get her hopes up.

He came back in the room, then straightened the light blanket over her. Suddenly he put his hand under her chin, making her look at him. "Why didn't you tell me you met with your father?"

Even feeling sick didn't stop the tingle that shot through her at his touch. "You're relentless, aren't you?"

"When I want something, yes."

She scarcely dared to breath. "And what do you want, Brant?"

"A straight answer."

She noted that's what he wanted from *her,* yet *he* wasn't giving any himself.

"You don't own me," she said quietly, feeling they were walking on dangerous ground. "Is that straight enough for you?"

He dropped his hand from her chin, then moved back from her, his expression in-scrutable. "Get some rest. I'll stay and make sure you're okay."

"There's no need."

"Yes, there is." He left the room without further explanation.

Kia woke a couple of hours later and the nausea had gone, though she still felt a little headachy.

"I see you're awake," Brant said, lounging against the doorway.

She jumped in fright, then let out a slow breath as her gaze went over him. At least there was nothing wrong with her eyes. She could still appreciate how handsome he was. "You stayed?"

"I had to make sure you didn't collapse again."

"I didn't collapse the first time."

"No, but you would've if I hadn't been here to help you inside the house."

Her mouth tightened. "Perhaps if I hadn't been accosted in the driveway I would have been inside before I felt sick."

He straightened and walked toward her. "Don't hide anything from me, Kia. You'll find it's not worth it in the long run."

Suddenly she felt too weak to argue. Anyway, she couldn't tell him she loved him, no matter what. He wouldn't want to know. Not after his reaction last night when he'd held himself back from her. *That* more than anything proved he wasn't ready for a serious relationship.

As if satisfied that he'd gotten his message

across, he walked over to the window and looked out. "I think we should go away for a few days."

She blinked in surprise. "Wh-what? With you?"

He turned to face her. "It had better not be with anyone else," he drawled.

The thought of having Brant to herself sounded wonderful. "Do you have a place in mind?"

"I have a house in the wilderness about an hour's drive south of here. I like to escape there every so often. It has enough luxuries to keep any woman happy."

Her bubble burst. How many other women had he taken to this house of his? "Sounds fine to me," she said stiffly.

His expression softened. "Kia, I've never taken another woman there, I promise. I want to get *away* from people when I go there."

Relief filled her. "When do you plan on going?"

"Tomorrow, if you're up to it. I have a couple

of things to finish first, then we'll leave mid-afternoon. You just stay in bed and get yourself better. I'll swing by and pick you up around two."

For once, she would do what she was told. She didn't want anything spoiling these few precious days away with the man she loved. It would be moments like those she would always treasure.

The next morning Kia felt more alive than she'd ever been. All lingering nausea had disappeared during the night, and now she was ready to face the world. In fact, today she would *embrace* it. And for the next couple of days she would revel in her love for Brant. He need never know.

But first she'd drive into the office and leave a note for Evelyn, in case the other woman decided to pop in during the next week to check things over. Knowing Evelyn and the way she took her job seriously, she would want to make sure there were no problems.

And deep inside, Kia couldn't wait until this afternoon to see Brant. Her heart was full of love for him. So full she was almost bursting.

Her steps light and buoyant, she stepped from the elevator and headed down the hallway to Brant's office. Not only were her steps light but her whole body—as though she could float to Brant's office….

"You've got it all wrong, Royce," Brant's voice warned from inside the office.

A feeling of apprehension shivered down Kia's spine and she stopped dead. Royce? Wasn't that Brant's brother?

"So you deny meeting Julia on numerous occasions?" the other man demanded with all the menace of a tiger about to pounce.

"No, I don't deny it," Brant answered, his tone firm. "But it's not what you think."

Royce gave a harsh laugh. "Yeah, right. I heard her calling you on the phone, telling you she needed you."

"To talk. That's all."

"At a hotel?"

There was a moment's damning silence, and Kia's breath caught sharply in her throat. She prayed there was some sort of mix-up. She waited for Brant to speak, to explain….

"There are other reasons for being at a hotel," he finally said, and Kia's heart sank at his detached tone. What other reasons? *Please, Brant, tell us.*

"I'm not a fool," Royce snapped, obviously unconvinced, too. "I took away your fiancée and now you want her back."

"Don't be so bloody stupid. Julia loves—"

"Stay away from my wife or you'll be sorry. I don't care if you *are* my brother."

Kia felt as though her legs had been cut from under her. Julia had been Brant's *fiancée?* They'd been *engaged?* Had been contemplating *marriage?* And Brant hadn't bothered to tell her.

A lead weight settled in the pit of her

stomach. Dear God, it showed how little he thought of her. She was just another one of the harem. Oh, what a fool she was. An absolute idiot. Brant was no different than her father. She had believed Brant because she'd *wanted* to believe him.

She needed to get away. Be alone. She whirled around to leave, but then Brant spoke again. Her heart pounded. His voice sounded closer. He was going to come out of his office and at any moment he'd catch her eavesdropping.

"You're jumping to conclus—" He followed his brother through the doorway, stiffening when he saw her. "Kia!"

She swallowed, her gaze going from Brant to his brother. Somehow seeing Royce Matthews in the flesh made the accusations, the possibility of Brant's affair with Julia, more concrete. The younger man wore a business suit and looked rich and successful, and perhaps it was empathy, but in that split second she could see past the anger to the shadows under his eyes, to the bone-deep misery emanating from every pore of his skin. And she knew how Brant's brother felt.

Betrayed.

"Remember what I said, Brant," Royce warned, then strode past her and toward the elevator.

For a long moment Kia stared at Brant, trying to hold on to her composure. She heard the elevator door open with a whoosh, then close. And she knew this was the end for them. Utterly and totally. Anguish ripped her heart apart. The feeling was far worse than she'd expected.

Yet somehow, dear God, she had to face him with dignity. Experience with her father had taught her how.

She forced her expression to turn cool. "I have to get something from my desk."

Brant watched her in tight-lipped silence for

a moment. "You should have phoned. I would have collected it for you."

"Perhaps it's better this way," she said pointedly and saw his gaze narrow.

Finding strength in her legs was difficult, but she managed it. She stepped past him.

He put his hand on her arm, stopping her. "What's the matter?"

She looked down at his arm, afraid to show him her eyes…and the pain that must be there. "Nothing."

"So you're all packed?"

"No." She shrugged off his hand.

"No?" he repeated, his tone hardening. "Why not?"

She looked up, unable to stop herself from spitting fire. "I'm not going away with you, Brant. I've decided I've got too much self-respect to play second fiddle to Julia."

His jaw tautened. "I presume you heard Royce and I talking just now?"

"Yes."

"And you think Julia and I are having an affair?"

"That pretty well sums it up."

A sudden chill hung in the air. "Really?"

"I know what I heard." She went to spin away.

But he held her back. "What if I said you mean more to me than Julia ever did?"

A lump lodged in her throat. "Then why didn't you tell me about your engagement?"

A muscle flicked at his jaw. "It wasn't important."

"It is to me."

"Look, what Julia and I had—"

"Is none of my business," she finished for him. "Yeah, I get the point. I guess your brother does, too."

His eyes darkened. "Royce isn't thinking straight."

"Gee, I wonder why?" Her lips twisted. "Or

maybe it's because of his *drinking* problem," she said with sarcasm.

His gaze stabbed her. "You think I lied about that?"

"How else could you hide your affair from me?"

Cold dignity descended over his face. "I'm only going to say this one more time. Royce *does* have a drinking problem, whether you believe me or not."

Oh, how she wished she could. But the evidence spoke otherwise. "Then why didn't you tell him that was the reason you've been meeting his wife?"

His jaw went rigid. "There's more to it than that."

"More?"

His eyes flicked away from her. "That's all I can say."

Because he was guilty. Guilty of loving his

brother's wife. Just thinking about it squeezed pain through Kia's heart.

"None of this matters now anyway, Brant. It won't work between us. It's never going to work. I won't be second best."

Without warning, he grabbed her and kissed her hard. It was like kissing a stranger.

Until he softened it. And for a split second she turned boneless. The moment she did, he broke off the kiss.

"Does that kiss feel like you're second best?" he demanded, still holding her shoulders so she couldn't escape.

"Yes," she whispered. "That kiss was about *you,* not me."

He swore. "Kia, don't be so damn—"

"Let it go, Brant. Let *me* go. There's nothing more to be said." It was over. The end had come sooner than expected.

"Kia, it's not—"

Just then, the elevator doors opened and a

female voice cried out Brant's name. Kia heard him take a harsh breath, and her head snapped around to see a slim blonde fly past her and into Brant's arms, her face pale.

"Oh, Brant, he was here, wasn't he?"

Brant's arms wrapped around the other woman even as his gaze flickered to Kia. She saw a flash of despair in his eyes, and a hot ache grew in her throat. This man loved Julia so much he was willing to fight his brother for her.

Then he pulled back slightly and looked down at the exquisite features surrounded by a golden mist of hair. "Julia," he said softly. "We need to talk."

Tears glistened in Julia's eyes. "Darling, what are we going to do?"

Kia couldn't stand it any longer. These two people belonged together. She had to get out of there. Had to somehow put Brant out of her life. And her heart.

"Kia," he growled just as she was about to twirl on her heels.

She pasted on a false smile. "I won't stay, Mr. Matthews. I can see you've got your hands full."

Then she rushed toward the elevator. The last thing she saw before the doors closed was Brant leading the woman he loved into his office. Kia's knees buckled and she leaned against the elevator wall. She had never felt more devastated in her life.

Ten

Kia went straight home and packed a small bag, then tossed it in the car and drove off. She had to get away from here and she didn't care where.

She'd lost Brant. Lost him to the one woman she could never compete with. The one woman who had "mattered." He'd only wanted *her* body until Julia was free to love him again. He'd never wanted *her* heart.

But she'd given it anyway.

And Julia would soon be free. Brant and

Royce would fight over her some more, but in the end Brant would win, of course. Then he and Julia would celebrate with champagne and caviar and they'd make love with so much emotion it would bring tears to Julia's eyes.

Kia swallowed a sob. The pain cut too deep to cry. She just hoped Julia never found out what sort of man Brant really was. A man who loved one woman but thought nothing of sleeping with others to satisfy his sex drive.

Being at the northern tip of Australia, Darwin wasn't an easy place to leave on the spur of the moment, not with thousands of kilometers of desert between it and the southern major cities.

So for two hours Kia sat on Casuarina Beach and tried to think where she could go to lick her wounds. Eventually an approaching tropical thunderstorm made her look up, and she saw a billboard for one of the large hotels nearby. She made the decision to stay there for a few days instead.

She spent those days sitting on the balcony or walking along the beach, the breeze off the ocean providing a refreshing relief from the high humidity caused by the monsoon rains. In the evening she forced herself to eat in the restaurant and even managed to smile at people as if her heart weren't breaking and the food she was eating didn't taste like plastic. It all meant nothing without Brant.

But eventually she had to pull herself together and get on with her life. Tomorrow she would go home and pick up the pieces. She could do it. She had to.

But first she had to make her weekly phone call to her mother and pretend she was home and nothing out of the ordinary had happened. She was already overdue with the call.

"Darling, where are you?" her mother said the instant Kia spoke. "Are you okay?"

Kia's fingers tightened around the telephone. "I'm fine, Mum. Why?"

"We've been so worried. Brant's been looking for you and—"

She sank to the bed. "B-Brant?"

"Your boss, darling. Remember?"

Oh, she remembered all right. That's all he was to her now. One of her bosses. Soon to be ex-boss.

"He said you'd gone away for a few days but he didn't know where." Her mother paused. "We were really worried about you, sweetie. You never mentioned going away."

"It was a spur-of-the-moment thing, Mum," Kia said, feeling guilty for not calling sooner. Then she thought of Brant and her heart began to thump harder. "Do you know what he wanted?"

"He didn't say. I assumed it was another problem at work he needs your help with. He seemed quite upset about it, whatever it was."

Brant upset? He should be ecstatic now he was back with the woman he loved. She frowned. Or perhaps there really was a problem at work? Yes, that would be more likely.

"Anyway, darling, he asked me to call him the minute I heard from you. Where are you staying? If you give me the telephone number, I'll get him to call you."

"Mum, I'd prefer not to say," Kia said quietly. Brant would charm the information out of her mother if she told her. "I'm having a holiday and—"

"Darling, this isn't like you to just run off. I know you're a grown woman and all, and some things mothers probably shouldn't know, but I'll always be here for you if you want to talk."

Kia blinked back tears. "Thanks, Mum. I know that. I just needed some time by myself, that's all."

A moment's silence ticked by. Then her

mother spoke. "This isn't about work, is it? It's about Brant."

"Yes," Kia murmured. She took a shaky breath. "But please don't say anything to him. I'll call him shortly to see if there really is a problem at work. And I'll be going home tomorrow anyway. I'll call you then. I might even come down to Adelaide for a week after that." Suddenly she needed to go home. It would be for the best. Her mother, more than anyone, would understand her pain.

"Darling, you're always welcome here. You know that. Please call me tomorrow. I'll worry otherwise."

"I promise."

"And call Brant now. It may be important."

"I will." Kia hung up the telephone and stared at the wall. So he was upset, was he? Did he think she'd do something crazy just because he loved another woman? She wasn't that stupid. She was heartbroken, but life would go on.

Taking a deep breath, she picked up the phone again and dialed the number for his office. He answered on the first ring.

Just hearing his voice constricted her heart. Oh, God. How was she ever going to forget him?

"Kia?" he said when she didn't immediately announce herself.

"Yes." She swallowed hard then cleared her throat. "Yes, it's me."

"Thank God!" He paused. "Where the hell have you been?"

"On holiday."

He swore under his breath. "You've had everyone worried about you."

Anger hardened her voice. "They wouldn't have been if you hadn't called my mother."

"I had to see if you were there."

"Why, Brant? It's over."

"Don't be ridiculous. It's far from over. Not by a long shot."

She gasped. "If you think I'm going to carry on an affair with you behind—"

"Look, we can't talk about this over the telephone. Tell me where you are and I'll come to you."

"No," she said with a catch in her voice. In the flesh, he'd seduce her with more than words.

"Kia, I'm beginning to lose patience." He took a deep breath. "Please listen. This is important. I need to see you. I want to feel my arms around you and—"

"My God. Isn't one woman enough for you? Go to Julia, Brant. She'll be waiting for you."

"Dammit, there is no—"

"I'll come to the office tomorrow. Until then, just accept that I'm the one who got away. Goodbye, Brant."

"Kia, don't hang up. I'll—"

She carefully placed the phone in its cradle. Whatever he'd do to her would have to wait until tomorrow. It still wouldn't change her mind.

* * *

At exactly noon Kia stepped out of the elevator and strode toward Brant's office. She'd come straight from the motel, dressed in a mauve knit top, white jeans and sandals. She'd never dressed so casually at the office before. Never even contemplated it. It was kind of freeing.

Just like the letter of resignation in her hand.

Of course, telling herself she should be feeling free was different to actually *feeling* free. That would come with time. Dear God, she hoped so.

For now, she had to face Brant and get it over with. Then she'd put one foot in front of the other and march out that door and out of his life.

She squared her shoulders just before she stepped in the open doorway, but it didn't stop the impact of seeing him sitting at his desk while he studied some paperwork in front of him. He looked so handsome. So…Brant.

For one precious moment she didn't think she had the strength to do this. But she had to. For God's sake—for *her* sake—she had to stay strong.

He looked up and their eyes met. And in that split second her heart cried out for him and all that she'd lost. She had come so close to finding happiness, utter fulfillment, only to lose all chance for both. The grief over that loss cut right to the center, the heart of her. She would never be the same, not even close.

"Kia," he said hoarsely, as if feeling that same pain. But that couldn't be. He would have to love her to suffer the same sense of desolation she felt. Yet she knew he didn't. He loved Julia.

Somehow, from somewhere deep inside her, she found the strength to enter the room. "I'm not staying," she told him in a firm voice.

His shoulders tensed. A mask came down over his face. "Why not?"

"I'm only here for one thing." She saw his eyes flicker over her, and her lips tightened. "No, it's not what you're thinking."

A muscle began to throb in his cheek. "And what would I be thinking?"

"Sex. That's all it ever was with you, Brant."

Those blue eyes bored into hers as he stood up and walked around the desk. "No. That's all you ever let yourself *believe* it was."

She stiffened. "So it's my fault, is it?"

He stopped right in front of her. "Who said anyone was at fault?" he asked quietly.

She gaped at him in disbelief. "Surely you don't think this is how a relationship should be?"

He reached out and cupped her chin, looking deep into her eyes. "Just because two people fall in love doesn't mean everything runs smoothly, sweetheart. But that doesn't mean they should end what they have."

She sucked in a sharp, painful breath and jerked her chin away. Dear God, was he enjoying the wounds he caused by his affair with Julia? "In other words, I should just let things slide along as they are? Boy, you really take the cake."

He seemed to freeze for a long pause. Then he said, "Kia, did you hear what I said?"

"No! I don't want to hear any more. I've come to give you this." She thrust the envelope at him.

Moments crept by as he stared hard at her, and she shifted uneasily. Then his gaze dropped to her hand. "What is it?"

"My resignation."

"You're not resigning," he said softly, taking the envelope and tearing it in half, just as he'd done with the check she'd written out for him over the security alarm.

She pulled out another envelope from her pocket. "I thought you might do that. You can tear this one up, too, but it doesn't matter. I've already sent one to Phillip in this morning's mail."

"You are *not* resigning," he repeated.

She gave a short laugh. "Unless you chain me to my desk, I won't be coming back."

"Chaining you to your desk sounds a bloody good idea right now," he muttered, grabbing her shoulders and lightly shaking her. "Kia, you say you listen, but you don't actually *hear* what I'm saying. I love you, Kia Benton. I'm not going to let you walk out of my life. I can't."

Her heart lurched in her chest. "Please don't do this to me, Brant," she whispered. "I can't be your mistress."

His hands tightened on her shoulders. "I don't want you for my mistress. I want you to be my wife."

Her mind spun in shock. His wife? For just a moment hope blossomed. Oh, yes, she wanted to be married to him so badly she ached with it. But did he love her, truly love her?

Then she remembered Julia, and that hope shriveled. There was only one woman he loved. A woman who belonged to another man at the moment. Kia's heart plummeted even further. Is that why he was asking *her* to marry him now? Had something gone wrong between him and Julia?

Regret and pain at what could have been flowed through her, cutting deep. "I'm sorry, Brant. I can't."

His head reeled back. "Why?" he rasped in a voice low and raw with something that sounded like need.

She blinked back tears. "You want me, but that's not enough. It'll never be enough for me."

"It's more than enough. For both of us."

"You're wrong. I won't be a substitute for Julia. I can't," she cried, spinning away. She had to get out of there before she fell apart. Before she let herself be taken on any terms.

"Stay."

His plea stilled her. Slowly she turned. Their gazes met for a long moment that seemed to last for eternity. She searched to the depth of his soul in those dark eyes, wanting to believe he loved her yet afraid to accept that the pain, the longing in his eyes, was real and not her imagination. She shook her head. No, she was too emotional to trust her judgment right now.

She was about to turn away again, to really go this time, but all at once she saw the anguish in his eyes and her legs refused to move. Brant wasn't a man to show his emotions and certainly not his vulnerability. Yet here he was showing that very thing. Hope and wonder bubbled inside her. Dare she believe? Could she believe in him? In herself? Her judgment?

She needed to stay rational. She needed to find out more about his relationship with the other woman before deciding. "What about Julia?"

The intensity of his gaze remained strong on her face. "She's already a wife. To Royce."

"But…you love her. You said things don't always run smoothly for people in love."

He took a step toward her and slipped his arms around her waist. "I meant *us*. I love *you*."

Yet something held her back, kept her from trusting him. An inner fear that she would still be second best, runner-up to Julia. He may think he loved *her* in a moment of madness, but for how long? Today? Tomorrow? For how many tomorrows would he love her? Would he secretly long for Julia, long to have her in his arms, even as he held *her*?

She just didn't know. She drew in a ragged breath, trying to think rationally, to get some clear focus. The only way she would get any kind of perspective was to have space to think about what had happened. She had to think about Brant's words of love. So much depended on her making the right decision.

"I need to think, Brant." She started to turn away, pain choking her words at the shock on that handsome face she so loved.

He stopped her, his gaze intense on her

face. "You've got to believe, Kia. Trust in my love for you."

Something in his words got through to her this time. She didn't move, but suddenly she listened. Really listened.

A smile turned lovingly at the corners of his mouth. "Hear my heart, darling. Hear and learn." He put her hand against his chest. She could feel his heart thudding hard beneath it. And she could actually *hear* it as she looked deep into his eyes.

"You *really* love me, Brant?" she murmured, one inch from believing.

"You and no other," he said, his voice thick and unsteady. "I began to get an inkling when you were sick. You were going on about looking a mess, and I realized then I'd never tire of looking at you. That I would always find you beautiful, inside and out. No matter what."

Her knees wobbled. She felt weak and giddy all over. Finally she did believe.

Relief flooded her that she no longer had to fight her love for him. "Dear God, I've been wanting you so much. I…" She hesitated, still half-afraid to say the words out loud, as if all this would just disappear if she did.

His gaze filled with so much love she wondered how she ever doubted it. "I'm waiting."

She looked up at his strong, vital countenance, that firm mouth, those compelling blue eyes, that dark hair. "Oh, Brant, I love you, too."

He let out a slow, shaky breath that warmed her insides. "I know."

A soft gasp escaped her. "What?"

"Once I let go of the notion you were a gold digger…" His eyes apologized for ever thinking that. "I finally realized you weren't the sort of woman to get involved with a man unless your heart was involved, too. You see, I didn't listen to my heart either."

She moved closer, loving the feel of his hard

body against her own. She'd never get enough of him. "Kiss me, darling."

His eyes darkened and he obliged her by doing exactly what she asked. And then some. Their kiss was so slow and deep it spoke more than words ever could.

When they pulled back from each other, she wanted to wallow in her joy. "Oh, Brant, I didn't know I loved you. Not at first. I thought it was just sexual attraction. It wasn't until we made love that it hit me."

His mouth curved into a smile. "You should have said something."

She rolled her eyes. "Oh, right. You would've disappeared off the face of the earth if you'd known I was serious."

He grinned and his love for her shone through. "Loving you isn't *that* bad."

"May I remind you of that in fifty years' time?" she teased, smoothing her fingers along his jaw.

"Definitely." He kissed her with a brief, hard

kiss that still managed to touch her soul. "I have some other news. Phil's decided to stay in Queensland with Lynette and become a 'gentleman farmer'. I'm going to buy him out."

She nodded, knowing it was a good idea for all concerned. "It's best this way. As much as I like Phillip, he isn't a good businessman."

"You're right." His gaze held hers. "Now there's something else. About Julia…"

"You don't have to tell me. I trust you completely."

"Thank you, sweetheart, but I can tell you now anyway. I couldn't before because it was Julia's secret, not mine." He brushed a strand of hair off Kia's cheek. "She has a child. With a previous boyfriend. She had him when she was sixteen, and her parents forced her into adopting him out."

Her heart squeezed. To never see one's child…the pain of it. "Oh, poor Julia."

"I never knew and neither did Royce. It was

only recently when the adoptive parents died in a boating accident that Julia found out where her son was. She came to me because Royce had started drinking and she didn't know what to do."

"Has she told Royce?"

"Yes, and he wants the boy. He's vowed to stop drinking. I know he'll do it, too. The first step is admitting he's got a problem. That was something my uncle would never do."

His brother's willingness to get his drinking under control was one good thing, at least. "How does Royce feel about you and Julia now? You'll always have a past together."

"Let's just say I convinced him I have other interests," he said, pulling her hips closer so she could feel his arousal.

Her breath hitched in her throat. "Uh…other interests?"

His gaze dropped to her mauve knit top. In one swift motion he stepped back, took hold of the hem and lifted it over her head, leaving her in her black bra and white jeans.

"Are you seducing me, Mr. Matthews?" she said huskily.

He ran a finger along the tops of her breasts. "Do you *want* to be seduced, Ms. Benton?"

"Hmm…no, I don't think so." Quickly she moved away and hurried to lock the door. Then she pocketed the key and turned to face him with a wicked smile. "This time I want to be the *seducer.*"

His eyes filled with a slow, sexy gleam that would always stir her senses. And her heart. "You realize this is an office, young lady."

"Oh, so that's what that big wooden desk is for. And that leather chair." She strolled toward him and slipped her hand in his. "Come and sit down, Mr. Matthews, and let me take note."

* * * * *